WORSE GUY

A SCIFI VILLAIN ROMANCE

RUBY DIXON

Cover Design by: Kati Wilde

Edits by: Aquila Editing

❀ Created with Vellum

For everyone that couldn't get enough of Mycrul's story...I hope you like Victor's just as much!

WORSE GUY

Crulden the Ruiner is the most dangerous gladiator in the galaxy.

I'm his clone - equally ugly, equally dangerous, and just as feared. I'm also being held captive, since no one trusts a creature like me to be let loose.

A curvy, determined human named Bee doesn't think I'm a creature, though. In fact, she thinks I just need a guide. She's got half the males on this planet eating out of her hand, and she's confident she can do the same with me.

The managing little female has no idea what she's in for. I'm not some fool to be led around by my tail. But...the champion in me loves a challenge.

A champion also wants to win a prize. So I tell Bee I'll go along with her plans if she kisses me...right on my tusk-filled mouth.

I never expected her to say yes...

A NOTE FOR SENSITIVE READERS

I'm trying to become better at notifying readers of potential triggers in the books I write. These are the ones that immediately came to mind, but if you find something you feel I've missed and could potentially be upsetting, please do let me know!

SPOILER ALERT SPOILER ALERT SPOILER ALERT SPOILER ALERT SPOILER ALERT SPOILER ALERT SPOILER ALERT SPOILER ALERT SPOILER ALERT

- Captivity (both on screen and in character pasts)
- Self-harming
- Mentions of past trauma/abuse
- Mentions of sexual trauma
- Violence (both on screen and in character pasts)

SPOILERS OVER SPOILERS OVER SPOILERS OVER SPOILERS OVER SPOILERS OVER SPOILERS OVER

1

BEE

"Thank you for seeing me, sir." I give First Rank Novis a cheery smile as I stare up (and up and up) at him. The mesakkah guardsman looks very severe. His horns are capped with plain metal, his face is all disapproving blue angles, and his hair is slicked back and tied in a tight knot at the base of his skull. Even his uniform is plain. It's black, with one insignia that I think is Lord va'Rin's personal symbol, but other than that and the squiggles on his shoulder that denote his rank, he could be a janitor. The mesakkah favor plain, functional clothing, and so does this guy. Doesn't matter. I give First Rank Novis my sweetest look. His title's a little weird, but I suspect it's something like a space version of a sergeant. Judging by the stiff demeanor, I think I'm right. I do my best to look darling and helpless and human. "But I was really hoping to speak to Lord va'Rin. Riffin said—"

The starchy-looking officer clasps his hands behind his back and frowns down at me, the horns on his head making him seem downright intimidating. It's been years and I'm still not used to the sheer size of the blue mesakkah. On Earth I was short, at just an inch under five foot, but here I'm positively squat. I'm a footstool. A cute, fluffy little human footstool that no one takes very seriously. Including First Rank Novis. He gazes down at me as if I'm a pesky fly bothering him. "Lord va'Rin is very busy."

"Well, yes, I know. Goodness, aren't we all?" I chuckle at my own joke. "But I really do need to see him. It's about a job." I smooth my hands down my nicest tunic (which really isn't all that nice) and resist the urge to thread my fingers through my curls. "Riffin said that he could get me in to see you, and that you could pass my message on to Lord va'Rin and his lovely wife."

My—boyfriend? Sure, we'll call him boyfriend—Riffin would probably be upset to know I keep reminding his senior officer that it was his idea for me to talk to his superior. Even now, Riffin stands just outside the office and I can only imagine what he's thinking. Silly, soft Bee getting another idea in her head. But I know this is a good one, and that's why I'm here today instead of at the laundry center, washing a jillion sheets for people with loads more credits than me.

So I keep smiling, because I know I'm right, and you can win a lot more people with a smile than a frown. I'm banking on the fact that mesakkah find humans absolutely adorable—like puppies, except uh, some of them want to fuck us, so I guess not exactly like puppies after all. Doesn't matter. I'm banking on being cute. I'd flutter my lashes if I wasn't worried it'd come across as weird.

"Human female, we do not have the time for requests right now," he practically snarls at me. "We have over a hundred new arrivals that must be processed, along with some cases that require special handling. You should go and tend to your farm and be thankful Lord va'Rin cares for humans at all."

Right. The downside of looking adorable and small is that no one takes you seriously. "I don't have a farm, sir. Allergies." I put a finger on the tip of my nose and wiggle it. "There's something in the soil here that makes me break out in hives, but I'm fine if I stay in town. I'm actually a laundress." If my mother knew that all of those years of college debt were going to end up with me doing alien laundry, she'd probably need to lay down. It's not like I chose it. I'm just rolling with the punches. I decide to roll right into my request, since dancing around it isn't going to get me anywhere. "So let me tell you why I think Port needs a social worker for the humans and why I should be that person."

"Not today," First Rank Novis says. He picks up a data pad off his desk, tucks it under his arm, and then heads out of his office as if we weren't right in the middle of a conversation. Rude.

I follow after him, determined to get my say. I pass by my boyfriend—Riffin—who frowns at me as his supervisor sweeps past. He frowns even more when I trot after Novis and begin speaking. "I realize you're a very busy man, er, alien, First Rank Novis. Riffin says that you've been tasked with handling a lot of the initial settling of the humans, and that's where I think you need me."

He snorts, marching down the hall. His tail flicks once and he looks over his shoulder at Riffin, who is following behind with a worried look on his face. "I have only told her the basics, sir. Nothing secret. I would never compromise the security of this place." Riffin grabs my arm, but I jerk free and continue after them. "The human—"

"My name is Bee," I say, because I don't like being referred to as "the human," especially by a guy that expects me to kiss him later. I worm out of his grip and trot after Novis. "And I point out that you need a social worker because you need a liaison that understands humans and that humans won't be afraid to talk to. Did you know that three farms were attacked last month?"

Novis sighs and keeps on walking, ignoring me.

I keep right on talking. "And did you know that Regina over at farm district thirteen had her farm attacked by poachers? She got married fast so no one could steal her property, but it wasn't a choice she should have had to make. And Lexi—she's in farm district eight, by the way—says she went to the doctor last week for cramps and he refused to treat her because he thought she was making it up to get medication."

Their steps speed up, and with a huff, I walk even faster to keep up.

"Bee," Riffin hisses at me, trying to get my attention.

I ignore him and raise my voice a bit more. "Lexi ended up having a tumor in her uterus that was causing excessive bleeding and she almost died. How do you think Lord va'Rin would have liked that if you had a human die on your watch?"

The mesakkah officer stops so suddenly that I crash into his backside. His tail swivels and smacks me across the shoulder.

"Sorry," I breathe, forgetting to be effervescent for a brief moment.

"You think humans are in danger of dying?" Novis practically snarls at me. "And that you can save them?"

Riffin puts his hands on my shoulders. "Come on, Bee—"

"No, that's not what I'm saying at all," I manage, detangling myself from Riffin's grasp. Seriously, when I need an interfering mesakkah boyfriend to take point for me, I'll ask. I get that Riffin is trying to be helpful, but this isn't the time. "I'm saying that humans are afraid to stand up to aliens because they're big and scary and we're small and fragile." When that gets his attention, I put on my happiest smile. "They need a friend to talk to. A go-between that isn't afraid to speak up on their behalf."

"A friend," he says thoughtfully, and then really, really stares at me hard. "You think this solves all their problems if I hire you?"

I can practically hear the sneer in his voice, but I choose to ignore it. "It certainly can't hurt. Let me prove myself to you."

That elicits a smile from Novis. "Fine. You want to prove yourself to me? You can be the advocate for one particular refugee I have in mind. If this works, I'll hire you as a full-on liaison."

I clasp my hands together with delight. "That's perfect! Thank you so much! You won't regret this!"

"No, but you might," Novis says, flicking his finger over his data pad. "The refugee is Crulden."

I don't recognize the name, but Riffin does. He stiffens and steps between me and his boss. "Sir, no. Bee is far too delicate to work with him—"

"Lord va'Rin said that the other one"—his voice drops low —"showed great success and willingness to cooperate once there was a female involved. We can try this."

"Sir, she's *my* female." Riffin sounds pissed. "I don't want her anywhere near him. It's out of the question."

Well, I'm pissed too. Riffin isn't my owner, and I hate that these two twits are talking over me as if I'm not even here. "I want the job," I say stubbornly. "I can work with anyone." The refugee is male, so he's probably a little unruly, but it's nothing I can't handle. A little sweetness and a willingness to listen go a long way. I can have this guy eating out of my hand in a week. "I'll work with this Crulden."

"Sir," Riffin says, leaning in. He gives his officer a mean-ingful look and they eyeball each other. "It's dangerous."

"We'll have her well protected, cadet," Novis promises my boyfriend. "Don't worry. She'll fail at taming him, and she'll leave both of us alone about this job request."

"I can hear both of you," I exclaim. "I'm not deaf, just short!"

Novis ignores me and gives Riffin a smug smile. "She has a

week. If he doesn't show improvement in that week, the entire thing is off. Then we all walk away winners." He nods at my mesakkah boyfriend, barely glances at me, and then marches down the hall with his data pad. "Have her at the security barracks first thing in the morning. No perfumes. Crulden has a sensitive nose." He pauses and looks back at Riffin. "And no mating."

I make a sound of protest that's ignored by everyone. "We're just dating!"

I'M SO mad at Riffin for interfering that I give him the silent treatment for the rest of the day, and when he tries to comm me that night, I ignore him again. Here I am, trying to be a bastion of cheerfulness and they acted like I was as dumb as a stump. I'm determined to show them, though.

They think I'm going to fail at helping this refugee—this Crulden—but they don't know just how determined humans can be. Riffin calls me repeatedly throughout the night, but I know he wants the kiss I promised in exchange for him getting me a meeting with his boss. Ugh. Riffin is sweet enough, and handsome, but he's a terrible kisser and does nothing for me in the slightest. I've never been a particularly sexual creature, and the few rounds of sex I've had were uninspiring, to say the least. That hasn't changed now that I'm surrounded by aliens at all turns. I know some women find happiness with aliens and there are some happy with their husbands. It's one reason why I've agreed to "date" Riffin. I don't want to be a laundress forever and Riffin wants a human mate. We've had a few dates in Port and every time I try to break it off with him because I'm not feeling it (and I'm really, really not), Riffin insists I give him another chance.

I know we're mutually using each other. I know he likes the

"street cred" he gets from the other guardsmen that work at Lord va'Rin's estate. They don't like that the port custodians—militia soldiers of low rank sent to police Port itself—have good relationships with the human females and one's even mated. It's a pissing war to see who can get a human mate first, and Riffin is determined to win. I need to shut it down and tell Riffin he deserves better than a mate who gets grossed out by the thought of kissing him, and I was just about to...except I needed to talk to his commander.

And I've promised a kiss. With tongue. I try not to shudder at the thought. Last time we did that, Riffin blasted his tongue in my mouth so hard I thought I'd choke. It was not fun, and I'm definitely not looking forward to this next round.

But that's something to worry about some other time. I'm going to focus on my job with this Crulden guy, and I'm going to rock it. I don't know if he's alien or just a scarred and somewhat feral human, so I try to prepare that night every way I can. I take a long shower using unscented soaps and pull out a tunic and leggings made of subtle colors, in case brighter shades bother him. I braid my hair back and practice smiling without showing teeth. I dig through my box of "human stuff" looking for the only reading material I have—a comic book in French—and write down lists of songs I can remember from Earth. Music is sometimes a good memory cue, and I want to go in with all the tools I can.

I get a good night's sleep, and when I wake up in the morning, I'm rested, recharged, and ready to go. I dress quickly and head downstairs for breakfast. The boardinghouse at Port is fairly empty right now. It's me and one other woman, a new white woman named Melanie with blonde hair and a bright smile. She arrived last week and is waiting for a farm to be prepared for her. Melanie beams at me from the kitchen table when I arrive, handing me a bowl. "Good morning! You look happy."

"I'm starting a new job today," I tell her. "Social work. I'm helping with a test case and then once I ace that, I'm going to see about helping all the new settlers here."

"That sounds exciting." Melanie's eyes go wide. "What kind of test case?"

"Don't know," I admit. "Some gentleman the garrison has in quarantine because he's not adjusting well." I pile my bowl full of the grain-like porridge mixed with fruit. It's the breakfast here every day, and while it's not exciting, it's food. I remember far too many nights in alien "livestock" pens where we had to fight over small portions, and I'm grateful for whatever we get here. I thump down next to Melanie and begin to eat quickly. "Riffin should be here to pick me up soon."

Melanie gives me a dreamy look, propping her chin up on one hand. "You've really got it all coming together, Bee. You're so lucky."

Am I? Or am I just determined to hustle until it all makes sense? I'm not entirely sure, but I know I can't sit around and wait for the universe to do me any favors. It's already shown me that won't happen.

2

ASSHOLE/CRULDEN

I watch the guardsmen skulk around the barracks, my eyes slitted. I pretend to be asleep, because they let their guard down when they think I'm not looking, or when I'm resting. It tells me everything about the soldiers here, and so I pretend to sleep a lot. My arms are stun-cuffed to one of the bars at the front of the cage, and I know it's so they can shock me into submission whenever they want. Thanks to my last master, though, I've built up a good tolerance to stuns, and now I just pretend they affect me.

And I watch.

Something is different about today, I decide. There's a lot of the guardsmen around this morning, their sweaty, nervous scents flooding my senses with the need to hunt. I could take that one, I decide, as one approaches the bars with my food. He's practically dripping with nervousness, and it makes me want to bare my teeth with hunger. He sets the tray down and slides it toward my cage, frowning to himself when it stops short a good distance from the bars.

I bite back a malicious grin.

The guard approaches, his tail twitching, and I remain very, very still. He watches me, hesitates, then shoves the tray full of meal bars again. Once more, it gets nowhere near my cage, and the male makes an unhappy sound. He rubs his head at the base of his horns and then takes another step forward.

One more, I tell him silently. Just one more step and then the hunt begins.

The guard hesitates, then leans forward and places his hand at the edge of the metal tray to give it another push. His tail flicks in agitation, and the moment it swings toward my cage, I act. I reach out and snatch it, jerking hard. The male loses his balance and stumbles toward my cage, and then I grab him. I sink my claws into his arm and when he screams, I bury my fangs in his throat to stop his howling. Hot, warm blood rushes into my mouth, better than a dozen of their dry protein bars, and I revel in the sensation.

Kill, my old master's voice says. Make it messy. Give them a good show.

I rake my claws down the male's chest as I tear at his throat—

The sizzle of the cuffs—turned up to max—jolts up my arms. I can ignore it and keep attacking the male, but if I do, I discard all of the work I've done to convince them that the cuffs work on me. I'm not going to give up my plans for a snack, no matter how bloody, so I release him, howling my rage, and jerk at the cuffs. I make a good show of it, just like my master taught me, and lick at the blood on my muzzle. The male stumbles away, clutching at his neck, and I resist the urge to curl my lip in derision at his moaning.

It's barely a keffing flesh wound. Pathetic. I suffered worse on a daily basis at the last stable.

They send another jolt through the cuffs and I react appropriately, then lick the blood off my chops. I wasn't going to eat the fool. I just wanted to maul him a bit. Watch them scurry. Have a little entertainment. I keep my eyes closed and pretend to be unconscious, listening to the guards race around the room.

"Again?" the one in charge states. "Who got too close to the asshole?"

"Abbik, sir," another male says. "They're taking him to the clinic right now."

The one in charge groans in frustration, and I just imagine how annoyed his face is. "That's the third one this week. When are they going to learn? You don't approach the keffing cage! Why do you think he's in one?"

"Sorry, sir. Abbik is new. I'll have him reassigned to outpost duty."

"You do that. He clearly can't be trusted with this." The male sighs heavily. "Today, of all days." His booted feet echo on the floor. "Someone come and clean up this mess before Riffin brings his female in. We don't want her screaming at the sight of the blood."

Screaming?

Female?

My senses prick with interest for the first time in days—weeks? I don't know how long I've been in this cage. Ever since they woke me up. I don't know who the new master is, or why he's letting his guards fool around with watching over me. I don't know where they're keeping the rest of the fighters, or what they plan to do with me. Probably fodder for a particular match. Wouldn't be surprised if it was a death-match. They're not acting like they know what to do with me, which isn't a good sign for my longevity.

So I have to be smarter than all of them.

I remain still as someone brings in a cleaner bot. The thing whirrs, squirting a harsh smelling soap that makes my eyes water. My wrists ache from the angle that I've 'collapsed' upon in the floor of my cage, but I don't move. To do so would put them on alert again, and I want to know what this 'female' situation is.

The floor is cleaned, but no one bothers to clean me, which is a shame. I'd love for them to put a hand on me so I can show them just how many limbs I can break in under a breath. There's blood on my muzzle and claws, but I don't suppose that matters. The female isn't for me. They never are.

I pretend for a while longer, listening to the guards as they go about their duties. Somewhere in the distance, the buzzer that indicates a door is opening goes off, and then two new scents enter the building. One of them is familiar—a mesakkah male who's been in here plenty of times before. The other is new and beguiling.

It's a female. A female that smells different than anything I've scented before. My senses prick with curiosity. That must be the female. It's a being, but the scent is softer and more delicate than the others. It's almost...sweet.

I wonder what she'd taste like underneath my fangs. Even her blood would be sweet, I imagine. I like the thought.

I can hear voices talking as they approach, and hers is more musical and pleasing on the ear. The male with her stinks of a herbal soap that he prefers to hide his body odor, as do many of the guardsmen. To my surprise, the female has no such scent at all. It's a welcome change, because some of the guards make my eyes burn with how much they enjoy their stinky soaps. I can't wait to get a good look at her.

In fact, the curiosity burns at me so much that I feign an awakening and get on my haunches the moment they step into the room.

The female is...soft. That's my first impression of her. Soft and vulnerable. She's smaller than I thought, as she stands next to the stinking guard. The top of her head only comes to the middle of his chest. Her form is all rounded curves—fascinatingly round teats, a round backside, and soft-looking arms with small hands. She is not mesakkah, I realize. They are varying shades of blue and hers is a cross between a pale gold and light brown. Her dark mane is pulled into a tight weave against her head and her eyes are big and dark as well. Unlike the mesakkah, she has no horns, no protective plating, no nothing to give her defense of any kind.

Is this...a taunt? Are they trying to show me the most vulnerable creature in the universe as a joke?

"Is that him?" the female asks, her wide-eyed gaze resting on me. "Crulden?"

Huh. Is my name Crulden? I thought it was "Asshole." That was all my last owner ever called me, and the males here do the same.

"That is your project assignment, yes," the male in charge says, moving toward her and the male she arrived with. The one in charge smirks, but the one at the female's side is not laughing. He looks very unhappy, and I wonder if she is his female. He does not like the thought of her being left with me.

I don't blame him. I wouldn't leave a thing that soft with me, either.

Her mouth falls open, her expression one of confusion as she studies my confinement area. "Why is he in a cage?"

The one in charge snorts. "Because he is a dangerous creature. Just a short time ago he attacked one of my guards that was attempting to feed him."

The female's brows draw together. I wait for her to show shock or terror. Instead, she focuses her little frown on the male in charge. "He's not a creature, First Rank Novis. He's a person, and if this is going to succeed, you're going to treat him like one."

That's...unexpected.

"He's being treated like an animal because he acts like one," the male—First Rank Novis—says. "He attacks anyone or anything that comes too close to his cage. He's violent and unruly. He destroys everything. Lord va'Rin wants him tamed without the use of medication since he cannot consent to it, but I'm not sure how it's possible. He's tasked my crew with it, but no one can get close enough to befriend him. He doesn't like males, and Lord va'Rin suggested a female. So now, we have you."

Novis gives her a thin smile.

"I see," the female says. The males look at her expectantly, but all she does is watch me.

I meet her gaze. She stares at me, unflinching. Of course she is unflinching—she is across the room and I am caged and cuffed. It is easy to be brave with two males and metal bars between us. I give her a toothy snarl, letting her see the blood coating my muzzle. Her scent does not spike with fear, though. "What sort of alien is he? I don't recognize it."

"He is a splice," Novis says flatly.

"What's a splice?" She looks up at him, all curiosity, and I admit, I would like to hear the answer to this, too. I have never asked what I am. I just assumed that all creatures looked different than me, but perhaps not.

"A splice is a genetically altered clone who has been crafted from multiple races, usually with the aggressive and dangerous traits enhanced. It's in an effort to create a superior gladiator that will win consistently for his owner. If not, the novelty of a splice at least provides good entertainment for those watching the matches."

The female's small nose wrinkles. "Is that what he is? A novelty?"

"He is a killer."

He is wrong. I am a champion. Bred and trained to be a

champion. I was created to succeed. To destroy, if I must, but most of all, to win. To conquer.

She studies me, her round face thoughtful. "So what races is he?"

The guardsman loses interest. "Why does it matter? He is a splice. That's all you need to know."

"Yes, but if he is born with certain genetic traits, it'll help me understand him."

"Born?" he scoffs. "I told you. He was created."

"Of course you told me," she says politely, her tone incredibly sweet. There's an odd inflection to it, though, one that makes me pause and try to analyze. "How silly of me to forget."

"Quite," Novis says.

The female's smile grows broader but does not reach her eyes, and I bite back a laugh as I realize what her strange tone of voice is. She thinks they are idiots. She is humoring them. Mocking them quietly by giving them the words and actions they wish to hear, even if it is not what she believes.

I decide I like this female, even if she is working with them.

"Do you think he is part mesakkah?" she asks, her voice even sweeter than before. "I'm not familiar with a lot of alien races, but surely his coloring suggests that he has some of your blood?"

First Rank Novis gives a hard, unamused laugh. "Mesakkah? That thing?" He looks over her head and smirks at the other mesakkah guards standing nearby. "She thinks Crulden is part mesakkah."

They all laugh, as if this is hilarious, and the female's pretty eyes flash with annoyance, quickly hidden. Her gaze turns back to me. "But he's so strong and fearsome. I thought surely he got that from your people. Where, then?" She flutters her eyes, making herself seem helpless, and I bite back a laugh. She just insulted them and couched it in praise, and they are too stupid to realize it.

I watch as the commander straightens, puffing up with pride. "A common misconception with many of the smarter gladiators, but no. This one is a mixture of praxiian—that's the feline race—and moden, and a few other genetic tamperings I can't quite put my finger on. I doubt he's got any mesakkah blood in him at all."

Good, I think to myself. I want nothing to do with this fool.

"How interesting," the female says sweetly. "And the spikes he is covered with? The claws and tusks?"

"Who knows." Novis seems to be losing interest. He gestures for his men to bring something forward. "You'll be in this hallway while you work with him. See what you can do. Lord va'Rin is interested in his rehabilitation but if we make no progress, we'll have to let him know. You have a week."

"A week," she echoes, and watches as they pull a stool toward the windows that line the hall. "And I'm supposed to stay out here? What, do I shout at him?"

"You don't want to get in there with him, trust me."

"Why not? He's cuffed and he's caged. I'm not sure what you expect him to do.

"Neither one can hold him if he berserks."

"Berserks?" She tilts her head, gazing up at the captain, and for the first time, I realize how tiny she is. How unafraid. She is a small, soft thing amidst aliens that tower over her, and yet she shows no fear. Her scent has none. I find that very interesting... as well as the information they are giving her. Berserks? I'm not sure what they mean. Do they refer to my rages? I remain utterly still, in the hopes that they will continue to spill more of their secrets right in front of me, like the utter fools they are.

The captain nods. "Sometimes he loses control. You'll notice it when his eyes flood with red. If you see that, press the alarm, because at that point, no cage will hold him. His strength multiplies, and the adrenaline in his system surges to the point that he becomes a danger to everyone, no matter cage or cuffs."

"Then how do you calm him?"

Novis laughs. "Calm him?" He shakes his head. "We're doing good just to get out of the way. There's no calming him when he's like that. He's a monster. You call for help, and we sedate him with everything we have."

The female frowns at that. "I thought Lord va'Rin preferred non-chemical means of handling Crulden?"

"He also doesn't want his guards to die senselessly trying to help a creature that wants no help." The captain's face grows cold. "You have a week, like I said. If he kills anyone or anything —including you—we're going to put him down. I'm afraid he's costing too much in resources as it is."

"I see." Her tone remains sweet and she looks up at the captain adoringly. "Thank you so much for this opportunity. I'll do everything I can."

I don't know if I feel sorry for the captain, or the female. She sits on the stool, outside the window, and just stares at me, watching.

I close my eyes and pretend to sleep so I can listen to all their conversations as I normally do. If they won't let the female in the room with me, there's not much entertainment to be had.

3

BEE

*T*his is definitely not going as planned.

I keep a cheery, positive smile on my face as I sit on my stool and watch Crulden from afar. They've set me up to fail, and I'm not entirely sure how to proceed just yet. I'm still digesting, and as I do, I watch the dynamics of the group from my spot outside Crulden's quarters (aka his cage).

The guards hate him. That much is blatantly obvious. They refuse to go into his quarters unless they're forced to. Crulden sits in his cage, cuffed and silent, and the guards mill about in the hall, behind me. When it comes time to feed Crulden, they elect one of them to go inside. The guardsman then takes a few steps in, slides a plate of dry-looking squares towards his cage, and retreats out once more. I frown at this.

I frown even more when I notice the dirty squalor of the floors. I can only imagine how bad it is near his cage. Crulden looks like a damn mess, his muzzle a darker shade than the rest of him. He remains in the same spot all day, his hands hooked to the front of the cage, and I can only imagine how uncomfortable it is. My ass hurts after sitting on this stool for a few hours, but Crulden never complains or says anything at all. When his eyes are open, he watches everyone. When they're closed...well, I get the impression he's still watching everyone, just a bit more furtively.

He reaches for one of the food bars and has to shove his face into his cuffed hands to eat. Crumbs spray everywhere, and one of the guards makes a disgusted sound. "Filthy keffing animal. I don't know why we're even trying."

This is what he considers "trying"? Good lord. I watch as Crulden hastily shoves the bars into his mouth, and then even more crumbs litter his skin and the floor around him. No one goes to clean them up, or even offers him a drink, and my throat feels dry just watching this. I lick my lips, glancing at the guards. "When does he drink?"

The guards completely ignore me, nudging each other and sharing something on a data pad.

I clear my throat, getting to my feet. "Excuse me, gentlemen." I make my voice super sweet and girly. "I'm so sorry to bother you but can I ask a question?"

This time, my saccharine tone gets a response. One of the men turns to me with that dismissive smile on his face. "What can I help you with, female?"

It took me a long time to get used to being called "female" by aliens. Here, it's a replacement for "ma'am" and isn't meant as insulting as it sounds. Still, it sets my teeth on edge. I continue to beam at the guard, gesturing at Crulden's rather filthy rooms. "When does he get a drink? His food looks very dry." I point at the unused sink and toilet attached to the wall. "Wouldn't it make sense to let him free so he can handle his business?"

The guard shakes his head. "That would be a very bad idea. You've seen how he reacts to the slightest hint of freedom." He puts a hand on my shoulder, his expression affectionate. "But if it'll make you feel better, when he starts to look parched, we hose him and his cage down."

"Oh, I see." It doesn't make me feel better, but I've also learned to pick my battles. I keep smiling as I sit down on the stool again to watch. My mind races despite my calm demeanor, and when they get out a hose and spray Crulden down like he's a zoo animal, I bite my tongue. When they finally hose his empty bowl down to give him something to drink, I say nothing. And when they laugh about all of it and act like typical, thoughtless fools, I remain silent.

It's not that they're evil. They're just young and don't view Crulden as a person. To them, he's little more than a rabid dog they're being forced to watch until he messes up enough for them to get rid of him. It's clear that they're not going to give him a fair shake. Heck, if I was treated like this, I'd probably react with teeth first, too.

When it grows late, I stifle my yawns, continuing to watch over Crulden as the guards change shifts. I don't know what I'm hoping for—for him to talk to someone? To speak? To ask for his cuffs to be removed? He acts as he always does—he pretends to be asleep and watches everyone.

"You're still here?" Riffin asks from over my shoulder, startling me.

I jump, my hand going to my pounding heart. "Don't sneak up on me."

He frowns, looking at our surroundings. I'm in the same spot in the busy hall, the guards clustered near the door and chatting. Crulden's still in his cage behind a thick, heavy door. Riffin didn't exactly sneak up, but I wasn't paying attention. I've just been too caught up in trying to mentally solve the problem that is Crulden.

"You shouldn't be here late," Riffin says. "It's dangerous. Let me walk you back to the boarding house."

I want to protest, but it's clear I need to rethink my strategy. I won't be able to help Crulden—or get the job I want—sitting on my butt in a hallway, ignored by everyone. So I should head home, sleep, and come to this fresh in the morning. I nod at Riffin and get to my feet. He puts a possessive hand on my shoulder, and I glance at the cell (because that's what it is, no matter what they call it) one last time.

Crulden's eyes are gleaming slits, and I know he's watching as I leave.

IT'S a long walk to the boarding house, so I'm not entirely surprised when Riffin borrows one of the air-sleds from the guard house and gives me a ride home. I want to protest, but the truth is that I do need that escorted ride back home. Lord va'Rin is doing his best to make Risda safe, but wherever there are humans, there are people willing to prey on them, and sometimes it's just not safe.

I hate that Riffin's going to want something in exchange, though. He always does.

So I let Riffin guide me up to the doors of the boarding house, but when he looks expectantly inside, I steadfastly ignore it. I stop on the porch and smile. "Thank you, Riffin. I appreciate your thoughtfulness."

"How appreciative are you?" He reaches out and touches my cheek with his thumb. If I was attracted to him, I might find that sexy. As it is, it just sends a shudder up my spine. It's not that Riffin's a bad guy. It's just...I don't know. He's easily manipulated, which makes me think he's not that smart, and I like a smart man. Of course, it's that whole "easy to manipulate" that makes him the perfect boyfriend, so I suppose I can't complain too much.

He's also a terrible kisser, and just his touch turns me off.

His mouth tastes stale against mine and I've started to dread the kisses he feels are his right as my boyfriend. I guess he's not wrong. If he's my boyfriend, I should want him to kiss me, right? I shouldn't be relieved when he's too busy to be around that day. I shouldn't be holding him at arm's length.

So I tilt my face up, a silent invitation for a kiss.

Riffin is immediately on me, his thick tongue shoving through my lips and jackhammering into my mouth. I try to go along with it, to find some pleasure in his enthusiasm, but when he doesn't slow down, I go still and wait for it to be over, like usual. His breath tastes like old protein bars and I try not to gag when he gets overly slobbery. He just needs to learn how to kiss, I remind myself.

I just...don't want to be the one to do it.

Not for the first time, I think I should break up with Riffin. I know he's not interested in me. He wants a human as a mate, because several of the mesakkah men have claimed mates and settled down here. It's a status symbol to him, along with the promise of kinky alien (human) sex. He wants the other males he works with to be jealous of him and his status. He's eager to show them that he's special enough to get a human female. That he's part of some exclusive, dick-swinging club the guardsmen are setting up amongst themselves.

Too bad for him I'm not interested in sex. That need was killed years ago, when I was first captured. Now I just tolerate his caresses and dole them out as special favors and hope he doesn't ask for more.

At some point, it won't be enough. But for now? Riffin is happy. When I break the kiss, he beams at me and I do my best not to wipe my lips. "You still owe me from before," he says, ruining the moment. "When will you let me in so we can mate? Other males do not have to wait months for their female to accept them."

Ugh. I lose every ounce of sympathy I had for the guy.

"Then maybe you should find yourself another female. I told you I don't want to be rushed, Riffin. You keep pushing me and I don't like it."

Riffin gives me a woeful look that almost makes me feel bad. Almost. Then I remember he just whined about not getting laid and I don't feel so terrible about it. "Bee, I just want my mate."

Not me, specifically, I can't help but notice. He just wants a mate so he can flaunt it in front of the others. I've caught him bragging—and not in pleasant ways—about me to the other males. I know he's using me, and I'm using him, too. I should break it off, but tonight I'm just too tired and my mind is on a million other things. So I smile sweetly and apologize. "I know, Riffin. It's just hard for me. Give me a bit more time?"

"I've given you a lot of time already. I just want to know when it's my time," he grumps, but sighs and opens the door to the boarding house, gesturing I should go in. So much for chivalry, I think, as the doors practically smack my ass on the way inside. I should pay attention to my friend Lucy, who insists that the way to a man's heart is through his stomach. She's recently mated to an adoring hunk that works over at the port custodial offices, and has offered to set me up with a friend if I ditch Riffin, but I haven't taken her up on it yet.

Men are such work, sometimes, that the thought of having to train a new one is exhausting.

Thinking about Lucy reminds me that there's more than one way to get on a man's good side, and it doesn't have to be with kisses. Since this world is strongly laced with misogyny, I've adopted a "cheerful but somewhat idiotic" nature so I get what I want without pushing too hard. No one sees me as a threat, and it serves me well. I head for the kitchens, because I think I'm going to bring some baked goods to my new co-workers in the morning.

The more they enjoy having me around, the better it is for me.

The next morning, when I arrive back at the guard station, I do so with a massive batch of cookies.

Well, I guess they're more like scones. Biscuits? I know that most of the blue aliens aren't a big fan of sweets, so I ease off on the sugar and add nuts instead. The result is a chunky, textured, nut-filled unsweetened cookie that tastes terrible to me but everyone else snaps up with excitement. The men crowd around me with eagerness, and for a moment, I feel bad for them. They're all young, and I know they're like Riffin, taking these jobs because they pay well, are considered honorable posts, and so they can send funds back home. They're all younger than my thirty-three years, and right now, I feel like a PTA mom in charge of snacks.

Even Riffin forgets to be mad at me when I arrive with the treats. He beams benevolently at his co-workers as they dig into the cookies. "Play it right, and I'll have her make you treats every day," he tells them, like I'm a trained dog who's learned a new skill.

I keep smiling, even though I want to stomp on Riffin's foot in irritation. I take out a specially wrapped package and hold it to my chest. I gesture at the window into the next room over, where Crulden is being housed. "So who is going to give Crulden his share?"

That silences them. The guards stop, watching me.

"Crulden?" one asks, crumbs flying from his mouth. "Why d'you wanna feed him?"

I blink innocently. "Why, he's my job. And he's not a prisoner, right? He's being reformed, not condemned, so why wouldn't I bring him a treat as well?" I smile sweetly at them.

"After all, the goal is to integrate him into daily life here, yes? That includes the good things, too."

The guardsmen look at me as if I'm insane. "You want to feed him?"

One laughs. "Don't you like having hands?"

"Well, I thought we could do like you guys and slide his plate over." I flutter my lashes, and if that doesn't get me somewhere, I'm going to have to start twirling a lock of hair around a finger. "What can it harm, right? It'll make me feel so much better about doing my job."

They look over at Riffin, as if he's in control of the situation. Ugh. My "boyfriend" is frowning. "I don't like this idea, Bee."

"But I bet Crulden is hungry," I point out, and move to the window. I peer in and sure enough, Crulden is on the floor in his cage, but his eyes are open and he's watching me with intense eyes. "Hello Crulden," I call out in greeting. "I've brought you delicious treats. Are you hungry?"

"He's not going to respond," Riffin says. "He—"

"I could eat."

The voice is low and ominous, and his gaze remains locked on me. I shiver, because it occurs to me that he's not talking about cookies at all. I suspect it's all bluster, though. Wouldn't I do the same if I was locked up with a bunch of people staring me down and acting like I'm a monster? It's like poker, and he's calling my bluff.

Well, I've never known when to fold my cards. So I smile triumphantly and hand the package of cookies to Riffin. "Please give these to Crulden." When he looks reluctant, I pat his arm encouragingly. "Small steps to victory, Riff darling. Small steps."

"Right." Riffin doesn't sound so convinced, but a moment later, the reinforced door into Crulden's quarters is unlocked and Riffin steps inside. The awful stink of unwashed flesh and dirt hits me, but I do my best to ignore it, smiling cheerily as Riffin takes a few wary steps toward Crulden's cage and then slides the small, cloth-wrapped package toward him.

The moment it gets close, Crulden shoves the entire thing in his mouth, cloth and all. Oh. Oh dear.

Okay then, I decide as Riffin races back out of the room and slams the door shut behind him. Crulden chews, bits of fabric visible between his tusks. Tomorrow, unwrapped cookies.

IT'S the third day of cookies when I notice the men are getting careless. I make a comment about how Earth people like to have their cookies with milk, and practically all of the guards head out for the mess hall in search of milk to have with their treats. I'm left alone with one junior guard outside of Crulden's cell.

It's Riffin's day off or he'd probably be here with me, but instead, I've just got a stranger shoving cookies into his mouth and Crulden, double-locked behind his doors and no one to give him his treat. He's eaten the cookies every time I've brought them, and I know he's aware of when I arrive. This could be my chance to talk with him quietly, while the others aren't paying attention. It's hard to have a conversation with someone when you can't even enter the room, after all.

So I put Crulden's share of cookies into his metal bowl and hug it to my chest. I gesture at the locked door. "Go ahead and open that so I can give him his food."

The junior guard gives me a look of terror. "You're going in there?"

"I did yesterday," I lie. "And it was just fine. Now, come on. Open up." I give him an impatient look and put a hand on the door handle, bluffing my way in. This could either be the breakthrough that I need, or a really, really bad call. I'm running out of time, though, and if I can't make progress with

Crulden, I'm going to be doing garrison laundry for the rest of my life. Besides, I'm reasonably sure Crulden won't attack me.

Reasonably.

The guard hesitates for a moment longer and then makes a low sound of protest in his throat even as he types the code in to open the door. I watch him type, trying to memorize the keys. The alphabet they use is nothing like an English one and all the squiggles look the same, so I try to remember the pattern of his fingers on the panel instead. The door opens with a quiet buzz, and then I step inside.

The stench hits me like a slap, and I breathe through my nose as I take a few steps inside. "Hello Crulden," I say softly. "I've brought your food, and I've come to make you a deal."

I jerk backward when he hops onto his feet, pressing up against the bars as he glowers in my direction. He's terrifying to look at, all animalistic and looming. He's enormous, and the spikes that cover his arms and back look deadly, as do the wet tusks that jut from his mouth and frame his ugly face. His nostrils flare and his eyes narrow as he watches me.

"I've brought you food." I set the bowl down at my feet and crouch on the floor. "But that's going to end soon, because if I'm going to keep this job, I need to show progress. That's where I need your help."

His eyes look fierce and alarming as he watches me. His pupils dart and I realize for the first time that his gaze is so unnerving because his eyes are like a cat's. He doesn't even look at the bowl, just watches me.

"My job is to help you become a part of society here on Risda III," I say, deciding to throw my cards on the table. "I have a week to show progress with you, and that week is almost up. If I don't show progress, I'll be sent back to the laundry and no one will bring special foods anymore. But if you tell me what you like, I can bring it for you. If you prefer fruits to nuts, I can bake something with that. If you prefer meats, I can figure something out. I would like for us to work together, because we're both kind of screwed unless this works out."

I take a step to the side, and his unnerving gaze remains locked on me. "Screwed?" he murmurs.

Of course he'd focus on that word. I smile, my expression sweet. "Yes. I'll be doing laundry forever, and if you don't seem to be making strides, they're going to put you back into stasis or keep you drugged permanently. If you kill someone, they're going to get rid of you. Understand?" When he doesn't answer, I go on. "You have to pretend like we're following the rules, even if you don't like them."

I figure if I can get him to pretend to be obedient, I can eventually work him around to actually obeying the laws. Baby steps, I tell myself.

"Pretend," he states.

"Like a game," I agree, whispering.

His mouth curls into a terrifying looking grin. "You're good at pretending."

I keep smiling. "Beg your pardon?"

Crulden's smile grows wider, and far more menacing. "Your male still hasn't figured out you're not attracted to him."

Uh oh. Someone's been watching me far closer than I'd like. I continue to wear my smile, even as I straighten and brush at the skirts of my long, belted tunic. "You're wrong. Of course I am."

He laughs, the sound raspy and unpleasant. "Are not. When you're around him, your cunt's dryer than my ration bars. I can smell it."

I blink, horrified. He can smell me? That part of me? I freeze in place, wondering if I should race out of the cell. I don't like that the first thing Crulden's mentioned is sex, but...he's talking, at least. "Our relationship isn't sexual, if you must know. Riffin knows I'm not interested—"

Crulden's eyes narrow, and I still get the impression that

he's amused as I kick the bowl toward him. "He thinks he can make you interested."

"You can't force someone to be interested." Why am I even talking about this with him?

He snorts. "Obviously."

The plate skids a few inches away from the slot in his cage. Close enough. I'm not getting any nearer. "Just think on what I said. About us working together—"

"I could make you come."

My throat closes up and I recoil in surprise. This...creature? No, it's a man, I remind myself. A man that's been bred to be a killing machine. He's watching me with those deadly eyes, and for the first time in my life, I don't have a chirpy answer. I don't know what to say. I swallow hard, then nod at the cookies. "Eat your food. Think about what I said."

"I don't want to play along." His voice is low, dangerous. "I don't want them to think they've won."

I pause. No one's winning anything, but I decide to couch things in terms he'll understand. "Look. We both know what happens if you break out again. If you hurt someone. They will not hesitate to put you down like an animal, and if they do, we both lose, understand? You can't play the game if you're dead."

He extends one nasty claw toward his bowl and hooks it on the edge, then drags it slowly toward him, the metal scraping over the floor like my nerves are being scraped. "What do you get out of this?"

"I get to keep my job. You get to keep your life. I think those are good incentives, don't you?"

"I'm a gladiator," he growl-purrs, his voice silky and alarming all at once. "I get a prize when I win. What do I win if I play along?"

"Very well. What kind of incentive do you want? More food? Better quarters?" If his freedom is too nebulous, maybe I need to offer something concrete. "Do you like plants?"

He retreats into the shadows of his cage, as far as the cuffs will let him, and his face is hidden from me. "I will think about what I want."

"You do that," I say brightly, and turn and leave the room. The guard locks the door behind me with shaking hands, and I thump down onto my stool, surprised that I'm not shaking as hard as my companion is.

I've told Crulden what I need from him. Now I have to wait and see if he decides to play along.

4

ASSHOLE/CRULDEN

I think about the female after she's gone for the night. When the majority of the guards clustered in the hall, shivering in their boots, go home and I'm left with only a few overnight. It's the best time to break out, and just like every day that I'm here, I consider ripping my cage apart and tearing off heads until I leave the building. To run and see how far I get before someone retrieves me.

Instead of mulling this for hours, I consider it only briefly before my thoughts turn back to the female again. She brings food treats, and while she always remembers to save some for me, I know they are for the guards. She's a sly one, the female, for all that her face is round and innocent, her voice sweet and slightly foolish, she is playing them all.

I have to admit, it amuses me.

I think about what she said. About how we need to fool them all so they think I am tamed. I hate the thought of it, but I am growing weary of this cage and these cuffs. When they bring out the hose and spray me down, I bite back a snarl of anger and decide I am tired of that, too. I am tired of shitting in a corner. I am tired of crouching next to these cuffs all day long. I am tired of a great many things.

This is not how a champion should go out.

Sitting in a cage, covered in my own filth? Cuffed? I should be in a glorious battle in an arena. I should be fighting to the death in front of thousands who call my name. Not this. This? This is not worthy.

And so I consider what the female said.

They will not hesitate to put you down like an animal.

You cannot play the game if you are dead.

It occurs to me that I can trick them, as she tricks them, to get what I want. I can pretend to be tamed. I can pretend that they have cowed me and defanged me. And when I am free, I can find new arenas, new competitors. Instead of the baked treats the female makes, I will give them my grudging obedience.

And they will lap it up like grateful dogs, never imagining that I have a plan in mind.

The female returns in the morning. I smell her—and her baked treats—before she appears. Her scent is clean and fresh, with a light, musky scent to it that must be her natural human smell. It is a good one. I only know of humans as prizes offered in the ring, but I do not have a memory of ever being offered one myself. Surely a champion deserves the best prize?

I decide she will be my prize. When I get out of here, I will snatch this good-smelling female and claim her as my prize for putting up with these fools. I smile to myself at the thought. Her male's scent is on her skin, as if he has touched her, yet again, there is no arousal perfume, no sweetness of her cunt hanging on the air. He touches her and she feels nothing.

This makes me grin.

When I am done with her, I will make her cunt drip with

honey. She is a challenge, and it is in my nature to rise to any and all challenges. It is who I am. I am a champion, and so I must win this, too.

I will win it and rub the scent of her juicy cunt in her lover's face.

I like this thought very, very much.

❦

"You're in a good mood," the female calls cheerily through the windows of my cell. "Don't think I didn't see that smile. Do you want your cookies today? I made them with the Risda nuts you guys have here, but if there's a taste you prefer, I'm happy to oblige. Just tell me what you like."

She practically shouts this at the window, as if I am somehow hard of hearing. I can hear every word she says from three hallways away. I heard her male tell her that he wanted kisses, and I heard her turn him down. I heard them argue about it, and I heard the male whine like a petulant child.

I cannot wait to bring it up again, but I will need to be sly. I do not need the female to shut down. I need her to play these games with me.

So I tap the floor, indicating I am ready for my bowl, and say, "I like the ones with the round nuts."

She gasps, and the guards at her side panic, as if I have suddenly pulled out a knife. "He's talking," one cries. "Get Lord va'Rin!"

"Lord va'Rin is busy, fool. Get First Rank Novis!"

The guards race around like idiots. The female sits on her little stool and beams at me from the other side of the window, as if we are sharing a secret. I want to smile back, but I know my jagged teeth and enormous tusks will not inspire confidence. So I tap the floor again, waiting for the food (which is, admittedly, much better than the food the guards give me).

Her mouth forms a little circle and then she taps on the guard nearest to her. "Can't someone give him his food?"

They ignore her, talking amongst themselves and preparing their weapons, and a flash of annoyance crosses her face, quickly gone as she resumes her happy smile. The smile grows broader when the commander—First Rank Novis, as they call him—enters the hall and listens to the babbled reports of his men. She sits on her stool and preens as if she has just won a race. I want to laugh at the foolishness of it all.

The male arrives, all stiff shoulders and equally stiff tail, and glares at me through the glass. He does not like me. I know he thinks this particular posting is beneath him—he's said as much "in private," not realizing I can hear every word he says through the walls and the duct-systems thanks to my enhanced hearing. He is waiting for me to kef up, to slaughter someone so he can point to his lord that I was a mistake from the beginning.

Before, I did not care, but before, the female had not arrived with her suggestions to treat this like a game.

And that speaks to me, because I like to win. This is the way I can win...by tricking them all.

First Rank Novis gives me a long, searching look. "Decided to play along, have we?"

I bite back the urge to snarl, my tail thrashing in the filth at the bottom of my cage.

"Oh my," the female says brightly. "Look at how angry he gets when you're around. My goodness, he must view you as the biggest threat in the compound." She turns toward First Rank Novis and touches his arm gently. "And here he was making such progress. I wonder...perhaps he feels threatened by your strength? It might be better if you keep your distance."

It amazes me how quickly she manipulates everyone with a few words of flattery. Novis blusters and regards me, but in the end, he clears his throat and agrees that I seem to "react" better to the female.

They will give her more time to work with me, and as long as I do not show signs of threatening her, they'll let things progress.

I plan on letting them progress, all right.

THE FEMALE ISN'T LET into my cell again for another week. She's clever, always careful to flatter the guards into getting what she wants as she bribes them with treats and sweet words. She's patient, too. When she asks for something that isn't granted right away, I can tell that she doesn't forget it. Her mouth hardens ever so slightly before she curves her lips into another one of those achingly pretty smiles and then goes right on about her day. I find myself watching her probably more than I should, and I'm not the only one.

All of the guardsmen that are supposed to be keeping a close eye on me are fascinated with her. She is small and soft, with large teats and big, dark eyes, and an enticing scent. The guards comment on how "lucky" Riffin is, and when Riffin is not around, they speak on when they will mate and she'll come in stinking of his attentions. They don't understand how he's being so patient with a prize like her.

I don't understand it, either.

My cock stiffens and aches when I pick up her scent. I hide it, because the last thing I need is for the guards to notice that I like the scent of the female and to use that against me. But I am imprisoned and in a cage. For this Riffin to have his hands free to place on the female and he never touches her except to put his mouth on hers and take in her breath?

He is a bigger fool than I imagined.

After another week of sitting on her stool outside my chamber, the female finally grows tired of waiting. She arrives that day with a determined gleam in her eye, the stink of her male on her face and hands, but there is no arousal scent to accompany her otherwise. Interesting. She sets down her basket of foods and then clasps her hands, beaming at the guards who have been waiting for her arrival. "I think it's time we push boundaries a little, don't you?"

The guards look uncertain, glancing at her useless mate. He is sulky today, frowning at the female and in the direction of my chamber.

As if she does not care about her male's displeasure, she gestures at the door to the hall, the one that keeps me on the other side of the walls. "We're going to clean his chamber up today. It smells, and if it's uncomfortable for me and my poor human nose, I can only imagine how wretched it must be for you gentlemen." She beams at them. "So this will be a wonderful test."

"A test?" one says.

"Yes. I'm going to go in and clean up and talk to Crulden as I do. He seems to respond well to females, so I'm going to do what I can to make him comfortable, and the more he gets used to my presence, the easier he'll be."

Her male looks sulky. "I do not like this, Bee."

My ears prick at that. Is that her name? That short, strange sound? Oddly enough, I like it. It suits her. I memorize it, because I want to repeat it to myself later, just to taste it on my tongue.

"You heard what First Rank Novis said," the female replies, her voice crisp as she puts a large portion of her baked treats into my bowl. I've noticed that the portion she gives me grows larger over time. Does she know how much I loathe the dry protein bars they give me, or is this simply a hunch of hers? "He responds well to female energy. How else are we going to know if we're making progress unless we test things?" She smiles sweetly at him and picks up the bowl. "Now open the door so I can go inside."

I watch the male, curious to see how he reacts to her demand. He frowns down at her, this Riffin, and then relents a little. "Kiss me first."

Her mouth firms for a brief moment in that way it does when she's displeased, but she tilts her face up at him.

He clutches at her shoulders and slants his mouth over hers, dragging his lips over her mouth and stealing her breath. Curious, I watch him do this, because it is evident to me that she despises this touch. Why be mated, then? She remains still, waiting patiently, and when he withdraws, I see a gleam of saliva.

Did he...use his tongue on her? Is that why she hates it?

She gives Riffin a faint smile when he pulls away, and as the other guards make teasing sounds, she turns toward the door and discreetly wipes his taste off her lips. The male is patted on the back by a few others, and then someone types in the code to let her into my room. Immediately, they are on alert, watching to see if I pounce.

Pouncing is far less interesting than having the female visit. They need not worry.

The female—Bee—sweeps inside with confidence. There is no fear scent on her, which I find fascinating. Even when the guards make their way in to kick my food bowl over to me, they wear a hint of fear. She marches inside and takes a look around as if seeing my room for the first time. Her nose wrinkles, and I am certain she smells the urine and feces that never get entirely washed away with the hose. It is something I tell myself I am not ashamed of. I cannot go anywhere because I am cuffed, not even to the lavatory equipment attached to the wall a short distance away from my cage.

But I do not like seeing her disapproval of the smell and

filth in my quarters. They treat me like an animal, not like the champion I am.

Bee turns to look at me, the bowl propped up on her ample hip. She studies my hunched form, my filthy mane and skin, the cage I crouch in, day after day. "If I bring this food to you, are you going to attack me?"

"No, Bee," her male calls out. "You're already risking too much!"

I notice he does not enter my chamber. His fear stink fills the hall, though. He is worried for his female. He should be...I intend on winning her away from him. Just because I know I can.

Bee, the female, waits and watches me. I wait, too.

"Will you not talk to me today?" she asks in a low whisper, her voice pitched so the others cannot hear.

I grunt. "I am hungry. Are you satisfied?"

A tiny smile just for me plays at her strange, small human mouth. She looks around and then back at me. "This is a big cleaning job," she admits. "I can do it if having more people around is going to bother you, but I'd like to get things really cleaned up so you have a decent place to live. This isn't fair to you and I'd like to help. Will you let me bring in some cleaning bots or will the noise bother you?"

I jerk on the cuffs. "Can I have these off?"

"I can't promise that yet. You still have quite the reputation for attacking everything in sight. But if we clean this room up with no incident and you let me come in here without attacking..." Her smile brightens. "Then I can make a case for it."

Sometimes I suspect she is manipulating me as much as she is the guards. But since I have nothing else to do, I find I do not care. I am far too amused by watching her machinations. She continues to hold the bowl with my cookies in it, as if she is deciding whether or not she wants to risk moving close enough to me to set it down, or if she will kick it over like the others do.

I watch as she studies me, then straightens her shoulders and marches over to my cage.

"As a reminder," she says softly. "If you hurt me, you go back to square one. Or worse."

"I have no interest in harming you." I let the words purr out of me, making my tone as low and gentle as hers. "In fact, I know what I want as my prize. My incentive to play your game."

Bee straightens, her hands smoothing down her pale pink tunic that somehow makes her skin look a warmer shade of brown than usual. "What's that?"

I don't give her my answer yet. I want her to wonder about it for a while. Two can play manipulation games, after all.

THE NEXT DAY, the cleaner bots begin to make regular appearances into my cell. They make sharp, irritating noises, whirring as they spray soapy water onto the floors and get to work. My room is so dirty that they work for hours on end, and the sounds grate on my nerves, but I know this is another unspoken test to see how far I have come. The female is pleased with my progress, I suspect, and once the floors are clean, she moves her stool out of the hall and into my room, near the door.

"When do I get the cuffs removed?" I ask, because my back aches with the constant hunching.

"When can I trust you?" She lobs back. "Maybe you tell me more about yourself. Maybe we become friends, and then I can get the cuffs off you."

This female. I bite back a snarl of irritation when one of the cleaner bots whirrs past, spraying soapy water on the tip of my tail as it cleans the edges of the cage. "What do you wish to know?"

She tilts her head, regarding me. "Well, for starters, I

suppose we could introduce ourselves. My name is Bee. It's short for Beatrice, but that's too stuffy, so I just go by Bee."

I watch her. Her tone is casual and intimate, as if it is just us alone, having a conversation. Yet when I glance over her head, there are a half-dozen guardsmen lurking nearby, watching us. Waiting for me to threaten her so they can end me. It makes me not want to say anything, but I know she's desperate to prove that she can make progress with me, that she can befriend me and somehow prove herself to these males that all talk down to her. "You know my name," I say slowly.

"Yes, but I was wondering if there was something you preferred to go by?"

"The guards call me 'Asshole.'"

Bee's mouth flattens angrily. "Do they, now? Well, I'm not going to call you that. So you tell me what you like to be called."

I shrug. "Crulden works the same as anything else."

"Very well, Crulden. I'm glad we're becoming friends." Her voice drops to a low whisper, and I feel as if she's speaking to me and me alone. It makes my cock react. "You...they told you that you're not the first Crulden?"

"I'm a clone," I agree. I've picked up that much from the conversations in the halls. "That I've been bred to fight in the arenas and win for my master." My lip curls. "Except the master I've been given to keeps me cuffed in a cage."

"He's not your master—"

"Isn't he?"

Bee goes silent, and I know she has no good answer. This male who claims to have "freed" me keeps me locked up tight. "Well. The reason I bring it up is that since you're a clone of the original Crulden, if you want to change your name, you just let me know. I'll respect your wishes." She shoots a scowl behind her, through the window. "And I will *never* call you 'asshole.'"

I bite back a grin, because I suspect someone's not getting to steal her breath tonight.

5

BEE

*E*ven though I know we're making progress, it's still startling to me to arrive one day to find that half of the guards have been reassigned and Crulden's cuffs are gone.

I set down the enormous tray of waffles—I've found a piece of metal that creates a waffle-like stamp and it's a great favorite with the guards, even without syrup—and smile at the two guards at their posts. "Changes today, I see. Riffin didn't tell me."

Zathar nods, helping himself to a waffle. "Lord va'Rin came by late last night to check on things. Fair had a meltdown over how First Rank Novis was handling the situation."

My eyes widen as I pick up Crulden's bowl and wipe it clean with the apron I've taken to wearing, since I tend to do a lot of spot-cleaning in his room now. "Novis got in trouble?"

The guardsman nods. "Said he'd told Novis weeks ago that Crulden was to be shown that we're friendly, not that he was a prisoner. We were all quizzed on how things were proceeding, and Lord va'Rin was pleased with your efforts, not so much with everything else. Several of the men were reassigned and Novis is going to let you take the lead on things, per Lord's orders." He shoves an entire waffle into his mouth. "And no more cuffs."

"I see." My heart trips at the thought of the cuffs being gone. I'm not scared, but I wonder how Crulden is going to take the change. Will he be pleased? Or will he decide that now he's been given an inch, it's time to take a mile? I suppose I'll find out soon enough. I stack several of the waffles into the bowl, filling it to the brim since now there's extras. "And Riffin?"

"Reassigned to house duty. Lord va'Rin says he doesn't want you to have distractions."

I should be sad that my boyfriend won't be nearby, but I'm honestly thrilled. He's become more and more possessive and demanding lately. It's almost like he's threatened by Crulden, which is ridiculous. I can't wait to have a few days to just sit and talk with Crulden without Riffin's obsessive hovering. Crulden won't say much if he thinks others are listening in, and I want him to open up to me. I want to hear what makes him tick.

So these new developments? I'm thrilled.

I enter Crulden's room with the bowl and instead of putting it on the floor at the base of his cage, I walk over to him and hold it out. It's a trust exercise, but either Crulden can be trusted at this point, or it's all going to backfire massively. Either way, he deserves to be treated like a human being.

Or an alien. Whatever. Like a real person.

He gazes at my extended hand for so long that my nerves twinge and I worry I'm making a mistake. Then, he reaches out for the bowl. His wrist is red and irritated, the skin torn and scabbed. "My thanks."

A thank you? God, I'm making leaps and bounds today. I glance around. "I should have brought you a cup. I'm sorry. I'll bring one next time."

He grunts and retreats to the back of his cage, giving me space. It's like he's determined to show that I'm in no danger, and it just pleases me even more. He eats, and I sit on my stool quietly, observing him. His motions are a little jerky, and I can only imagine how tight his muscles were after being kept in the same posture for weeks on end. I think about those torn wrists and decide that not only am I bringing a cup tomorrow, but I'm bringing some ointment for his wrists. "Did you talk to Lord va'Rin?"

Crulden doesn't answer, so I assume that's a no.

"He's quite a nice man, though I've only talked with him briefly myself. The rescue operations he's running keep him very busy. Did you know his wife is human?"

He gets to his feet, holding the bowl out. "Water."

I'm not sure if it's a request or a demand, but I decide to think of it as a request. I get up and take the bowl from him and return it once I've filled it with fresh water from the tap. He tips it back and drinks from it, and I can't help but notice that quite a bit cascades down his chin, as if his lips won't close entirely around those tusks that jut out. I wonder if they bother him. It seems rude to ask. After he drinks his fill, he holds the bowl out again.

I refill it for him, and he drinks three of them before he's satisfied, which makes me unhappy. "I didn't realize you were so thirsty." The moment the words cross my lips, I feel like an idiot. Of course he wouldn't let on that he's thirsty. He's not going to ask for anything or show any signs of weakness. "In the future, I'll make sure you're brought more."

He shrugs, glancing over my shoulder at the guards at the window, then moves to the back of his cage again. "In the future, I'd like to be able to get my own." His strange, tusk-filled mouth stretches into what must be a smile. "Since I'm not a prisoner."

"You're not, but you have a reputation—"

"You mean the male I was cloned from has a reputation."

Well, shit. He has a point. "You can't deny that you've been violent."

"I don't deny it." That feral smile he gives me would be terrifying if I didn't already know he won't hurt me. He wants out of his cage, so he's going to pretend to be "tamed." I haven't really thought ahead of what happens once he no longer needs to "pretend," but I'm focusing on one problem at a time.

"Then you understand why you're being kept...under surveillance." I choose my words carefully. "You have to prove you're trustworthy. That you're more than just that Crulden and his past."

"Mmm." He leans back against the bars of his cage and regards me, rubbing his wrists the entire time. Good gravy, his hands are huge. I mean, all of him is huge, but now that his hands are free, I can't help but stare at their size. He could probably palm my entire skull. "I will always be Crulden to these people, you know. You're wasting your time."

"You don't know that."

He rubs his wrists, as if the answer is obvious.

I refuse to take that as the answer, though. I shake my head. "Lord va'Rin is very fair. You'll see."

"But you don't know him," Crulden points out. "You said so yourself."

"I know he's a lot fairer than a lot of the other people on this end of the universe," I retort, crossing my legs on the stool to get comfortable. Even though I'm very short and round, I can cross my legs comfortably, and I dangle one foot, flicking it back and forth as I think. "It's not necessarily Lord va'Rin's words but his actions. Everyone knows the story of him and his wife. He was given a human, and instead of just using her as a pleasure slave, he married her and gave her his name and the rights of his family line. More than that, he's opened up this planet to human refugees so they can have somewhere to go where they're treated like people."

Crulden's eyes narrow as he regards me. "A pleasure slave. Is that what you were?"

I flick my foot in agitation, glancing over at the guards. They're chatting to themselves as they eat waffles and aren't paying attention. Good. Normally I'd complain about the terrible job they're doing as guards, but this suits my purposes. "I don't wish to talk about it."

"The only memories I have of your kind are pleasure slaves," he offers.

I don't know what to do with that information. I want to scream, because of course he sees us as living blow-up dolls. They're not his memories. They were either implanted or left-overs from the cloning process, but it's not his fault that he views us as objects, just like everyone else. Maybe I just keep it clinical. Facts only. "My people are not space-faring. We've only recently started to explore our universe, and we haven't met alien life forms." I give him a tight smile. "The people on this end of the universe view mine as inferior and enslave us, even though it's against the law."

"The laws don't stop many," Crulden muses. "Especially not those with deep pockets."

Boy, he's not wrong about that.

He rubs his wrists again and tilts his head, regarding me. "Humans seem very..."

"What?"

"...vulnerable." Crulden holds a hand up, showing off dangerous, dark claws that tip each finger. "You have no defense mechanisms. Your teeth are small and square. Your hands have no claws." His big hand slides up to one of the spikes that march along the backs of his arms and legs (and his back, as well). "You have nothing to protect you. Why shouldn't you be enslaved?"

I keep my smile cheery, even though I want to take that bowl of water sitting just outside his cell and dump it over his head. Is he trying to rile me? To get me to show temper? I refuse to rise to the occasion. "Because enslaving people is disgusting and immoral. You cannot own another sentient being."

He snorts, and the sound is amused. "No wonder these people think humans are stupid."

"Are you trying to make me angry, Crulden?"

"Yes," he says bluntly.

"Why?"

"We are arguing. I want to win." He gives me another toothy grin. "It's what I'm best at."

"Arguing?"

"Winning."

Interesting. "So your implanted memories are focused in regard to victory?"

"I suppose they are."

"Do you view all of this as a game, then?" I gesture at our surroundings. "A competition?"

His expression tells me the answer. He does.

That could be problematic. "And what will you do if you find there's nothing—or no one—to fight? What will you do if there's no challenge to be had?"

"There's always a challenge." His eyes turn to slits, but his expression remains amused, like he's enjoying our conversation. I have to admit, I'm kind of enjoying it, too. He's not talking down to me. He's not acting like I'm a precious doll that needs to be coddled and protected. He's not acting like I'm a victim, or that I'm damaged. To him, I'm a...challenge?

That's a little odd to think about, but I'm starting to suspect it's true. If he thinks of all of this as a game or a competition, then I'm either someone he needs to defeat or a prize to win.

I'm not sure I like either option.

"If you settle here," I point out, "you're going to be expected to abide by the laws. To be cautious of the humans that live on this planet, too. Most of them are women. Women that have been treated poorly. You need to understand that..." I cut myself off, because it feels like I'm giving information I shouldn't. Crulden feels a bit like a fox about to be let loose in the hen house, but doesn't he deserve to know what is expected of him if he settles on Risda? How he'll be expected to behave? I finish primly with, "You just need to understand how things are viewed here."

"And were you treated poorly?" His gaze is intent.

I clasp my hands in my lap and keep smiling. "I don't wish to answer that."

He grunts, and I suspect we both already know my answer.

AFTER THAT CONVERSATION, we don't talk about much at all. I probe to see what he knows, but sometimes Crulden just doesn't feel like answering, and I can't blame him. Sometimes the conversations feel like a sparring match, and by the end, I feel like I've lost a battle somewhere. It's obvious that Crulden is extremely competitive. He likes to have the last word in our conversations. He views everything as some sort of sport or challenge, and I worry that with the wrong focus, that competitive side is going to work against him.

The good news is that I don't think he's bloodthirsty. I think he's just bored and likes a challenge, and mauling guards was a challenge. He hasn't done it since I first started talking to him, and I don't think it's because I've made some sort of spectacular breakthrough with him. I think the new challenge is me, and I'm not sure how I feel about that.

Like I do most days lately, I leave the guard barracks late, and I'm not entirely surprised to see Riffin waiting for me.

"Bee, we've talked about this," he complains to me. "I don't want you staying late. It's dangerous. Promise me that you'll go home on time tomorrow."

His face is full of worry, his expression downright insistent.

I smile at him. "I always try to leave on time, Riffin. You know that. It's just that sometimes things get away from me. We're making such progress—"

"No, Bee." Riffin frowns, putting that possessive hand on my shoulder. "Listen to me. They're changing my schedule at work and I won't be able to escort you safely home if you stay late. Promise you'll leave before dinner."

I gaze up at my boyfriend in surprise. "Why are you so worried? If you can't give me a ride, maybe one of the other guards can." We've become friendly over the last few weeks, thanks to the bonding powers of pastries.

Riffin's face hardens, and he practically scowls at me. "Just do as I ask for once, Bee? Can you just give me one yes without turning it into a fight? It's like I have to struggle to get even a smile from you lately."

Hot guilt rushes through me. He's not wrong. Everything I've done lately has been Crulden-focused. From staying up super late to make batches of baked goods, to blowing all my savings on flour substitutes to obsessing over Crulden and getting him to open up to me, it's been my sole priority lately. I've really and truly been a terrible girlfriend in the last few weeks. "I'm so sorry, Riffin. I'm just...this job means a lot to me."

"I know it does, but you're wasting your time, Bee." He gives me a firm, unyielding look. "A creature like that can't be reformed. He's bred and programmed to be a monster. The sooner you realize that, the better off you'll be."

I fight back the wave of irritation his words send through me. He's lashing out because he's hurt that I've been ignoring him. I need to be a better girlfriend if I'm going to make this work. Of course, part of me doesn't want to make this work, and that makes me feel guilty, too. There are several women that married aliens to procure safety for themselves, and I know there's a lot of miserable marriages out there on Risda. Riffin is kind, and he lets me do my own thing, and he's patient. I should pay more attention to his needs, too.

"I truly am sorry, Riffin," I say, giving him my best happy Bee smile. "I guess I've been a little focused lately."

He gives me a tender look. "I don't mind your focus, Bee. I guess I'd just prefer it was on me and not on some lab-created thug." He touches my cheek and I bite back an unpleasant retort that wouldn't solve any of our problems. "Just promise me you won't stay late tomorrow. If there's one thing you can promise, do that? You're wearing yourself out."

It's an easy promise to make. "I'll leave early tomorrow, I swear," I tell him, and then tilt my face up for a kiss, because I know that'll make Riffin happy.

THE NEXT DAY, I'm mindful of my promise to Riffin, but when I go in the next day with my baked goods, the cage is gone. Instead, a new cot has been placed in Crulden's room with soft, standard blankets. They're the same ones I wash dozens of every day at my other job, and I know them well. Crulden isn't sitting on the bed, though. He leans over the sink, touching his face as he gazes in the reflective panel behind the sink that acts as a mirror. He regards himself thoughtfully, rubbing his jaw.

The moment I go into the hall, he turns to look at me. It's like he wants to see my reaction to the fact that he's now free. His gaze moves from my face to the stool inside his quarters, and then back to my face again, his tusk-filled smile growing broader.

It's practically a dare, that smile. He's wondering if I'm brave enough to step inside now that he's loose.

"That's a change," I say, clearing my throat as I set down the fresh batch of waffles in the hallway.

The guard at my side nods. "Lord va'Rin's orders. Of course, our weapons have been upgraded, too. If there's a hint of trouble, we've got stun settings on everything." He pats his blaster at his waist. "And Crulden agreed to be fitted with a stun collar in exchange for getting rid of the cage."

"Did he, now?" That makes me curious. I didn't notice it, but Crulden's so filthy and his hairy mane so wild that the collar might be lost underneath all that fur. "This is wonderful news."

"You sure you want to go in there?" the guard asks. "No one would blame you if you want to wait."

I glance over at Crulden, who leans against the sink, his gaze on me. The guards wouldn't blame me, but Crulden would know I was a coward. Whatever game he thinks he's playing with me would be done, and then what does that mean for our progress? Would he lose respect for me? I'm not sure why that matters, but it does. "No, I'll go inside. Nothing's changed as far as I'm concerned."

Crulden's smile grows wider, and I try to ignore just how many enormous, sharp teeth he's flashing in my direction. At this point I know him well enough to know that he's trying to intimidate me to see how I react. So I put on my favorite "amiable human" smile and fill the bowl with Crulden's portion of food, then open the door.

He straightens, no longer leaning against the sink, but remains there, his body tense.

"If you rush me, I'm going to spill this good food all over the floor," I say, letting my voice grow a touch tart. "And while it's much cleaner, I still wouldn't eat off of it."

The rumble of laughter he lets out tells me that I've "won" this round. "It's nice to see you, human."

I arch a brow at him as I approach in slow, measured footsteps. I keep all my movements around Crulden slow and deliberate, just in case. I don't want to find out the hard way that he has a prey drive. "You know my name."

"Bee." He breathes it out, and goosebumps flare all over my skin at the soft sound. "You never call me by mine."

Do I not? If I do, it's not often. I consider this. "I think it's because to me, Crulden is someone else. You're cloned from his tissue, but you're not him. So calling you by his name feels disingenuous because everyone thinks of him as a bad man. And we're trying to prove that you're a good one."

He takes a step toward me, and I notice his toes are clawed just as heavily as his hands. How did I never notice toe claws before? "You don't think I'm bad?"

God, how does he make me pause with every simple question? Why isn't there an easy yes-no answer to be found? Because the truth is—I honestly don't know. Crulden's becoming very good at pretending to be tamed, but I suspect that's all it is. Pretend. But I've done some reading up on the original Crulden—all terrible, terrible things—and it doesn't fit the man I know, either. There are stories of Crulden ripping off faces the moment he met people, or tearing women limb from limb at banquets...or worse.

So I don't think he's as bad as that guy...yet. But I think he absolutely could be if he wanted to be. He could be worse, if he wanted to be.

I swallow hard, thinking. He takes another step toward me, as if impatient to hear what I'm going to say, so I blurt out the truth. "I think you have the capacity to be good. I just don't know if you want to be."

Crulden grins at me again, and I don't know if he's amused or pleased or a cat playing with a mouse. "I guess I need the right sort of incentive. All boils down to that."

"So you've said before." I hold the bowl of waffles out to him, waiting. I refuse to back up or to show fear. If I let Crulden bully me, he'll absolutely keep pushing until he breaks me, and I'm not interested in being broken again.

"Gotta have something to look forward to," he says softly, and takes the bowl from my grasp. As he does, his fingers brush against mine. I bite back the gasp that threatens, but I'm startled at the small touch. His fingers are big and warm against mine, the pads slightly raspy as they brush against my softer skin. Goosebumps prickle over my body, and I blink up at him.

It's the first time we've touched.

Then I wonder, has he ever been touched? Or did they treat him like an animal the moment they pulled him from his pod, determined that he was the monster they expected him to be?

The thought makes me strangely sad. If everyone was constantly saying what a brutal monster I was, wouldn't I deliberately go out of my way to show them just how brutal I can be? Has anyone ever been truly kind to him? With this thought rolling around in my head, I hold my hand out to him. "Would you like to touch me?"

His eyes grow hooded, his nostrils flaring.

Immediately, I realize what I've just said. "Hands," I breathe. "Hands. I wondered if you had been touched as a friend. I'd like to be that friend."

Of course, now I'm thinking very un-friendlike things. Shit. So, so many un-friendlike things. He studies the hand I have outstretched toward him, my slightly curled fingers, my vulnerable palm. "Why aren't you afraid of me?"

"Should I be? Do you plan on hurting me?"

Crulden's fingers skim over my palm, and the touch is so ticklish and light that I have to bite back a gasp. He strokes his finger over the center of my palm, and I realize I didn't think this through at all. I thought we'd, I don't know, hold hands and squeeze them like buddies. This does not feel buddy-like in the slightest.

He places one big hand under mine and then clasps my smaller one between his. "You're as soft as I imagined."

I notice he pitches his voice very low, likely so the guards in the hall can't hear. I want to ask if he's been imagining me a lot, but I'm not sure I want to know the answer. "You can trust me, Crulden. I want to be your friend. I want to help you live a full, happy life here on this planet. Will you let me help you?"

The splice gazes at me, his hard eyes on my face for a long, long time, my hand sandwiched between his oversized, clawed ones.

"You're right," he finally says. "I don't like that name."

"Then maybe we'll pick a new one." And I give him my brightest smile.

6

CRULDEN?

I wasn't expecting to touch her.

In fact, I expected her to stay in the hall like the guards do. The moment the cage was taken from my quarters and the collar exchanged for it, they've been giving the door to my quarters a wide berth, as if they expect me to bust through and attack them. Which is fair, given I've done exactly that in the past.

She's fearless in her soft, smiley sort of way. It's like she's decided that she's going to be a warrior, but on her own terms. She fights not with claw and muscle, but with sweet words and sweeter smiles. It works, too. They all dance to her tune, and I do, too. It's hard not to give this female everything she wants. Not when she smells so good and looks so delicious.

There have been a great many changes in the last few days, but I like this one the best. I lean against the sink again, watching as Bee moves and sits down on her stool across from me. Just knowing that I can reach out and touch her fascinates me. Knowing that she is right there, that I can move over to her and run my hand along that soft arm? It pleases me...and it makes me hunger for more.

The male's scent is on her face again today, but her cunt remains dry. I have never mated, but I know what it smells like. Lord va'Rin came in with his pretty little mate when I first arrived, and although she was pregnant, he whispered filthy things into her ear and made her cunt fill with fragrant need. That taught me a lot, listening in to that conversation and her reactions to it. When a male arouses his mate, her body responds.

Bee does not respond to her male, and I cannot wait to test her. To see if she responds to me.

I know she will. I am a champion, after all. Why not in this?

I wonder what Bee's cunt would smell like if I aroused her with soft words? If I told her all the things I thought about doing to her body in the dead of night? When the lights are off and the guards think I am sleeping, I instead think about the aching heat of my cock, and how it rises when I think about Bee. The implanted memories I have are enough that I know the mechanics of mating, but I have no practical experience. Would she let me touch her cunt? Would she let me push my cock inside her?

She is soft, though, and I am not. I am barbed all over. It would hurt her. I have never cared about hurting someone before, but I care about hurting Bee.

"Well," Bee asks, crossing those thick, yet delicate, enticing legs of hers as she sits on the stool. "Have you given it much thought?"

My cock twitches in my trou. "All the time," I growl. "But mostly late at night."

Her head tilts to the side and a little frown crosses her rounded face. "Why at night?"

Because it is the only privacy I have, those moments in the

darkness when I can hide in the back of my cage and rub the heel of my palm against my aching shaft? "I do not want to be overheard."

"Oh." Bee leans forward. "Would you like your new name to be a secret, then?"

My name?

I suddenly want to laugh. Of course we are talking about names and not the violent longings I have for her. "I suppose it does not matter," I say, swiftly changing subjects before my cock hardens enough to tent the front of the loose trou that they have given me to wear. I touch the collar at my neck, because it feels strange against my fur, but not as obtrusive as the cuffs were. "What do you want to call me?"

Her brows draw together and she laughs, for once her smile real and genuine. "That's not how names work."

"How do they work, then?"

"You pick your name."

"Did you pick yours?"

The rounded swells of her cheeks flush with color and her scent heightens. "Well, not really. My mother gave it to me at birth. It was my grandmother's name, so she passed it down. But everyone has always just called me Bee, and I prefer that." She clasps her hands in her lap. "Your situation is slightly different. If you have parents, they're not around to tell us what they prefer to call you, so I think it's safe to say that you can pick your own name. Do you have anything that you like?"

I lift one shoulder in a shrug, then scratch at one of the spikes that pierces through my skin. They are scabbed up, and it itches. "Champion?"

"Um." She considers this. "Maybe 'Champ'?"

"Maybe not." I curl my lip with distaste. It sounds...cheery. I do not like cheery...unless it's her.

"Then give me another suggestion," she says, folding her

hands over her knee. "What about...Victor? Short for Victorious?"

"What about 'Ultimate One'?"

She giggles, her hand going to her mouth, and the sound is delightful, even if she is laughing at me. "I wouldn't be able to call you that with a straight face."

Her smile pleases me. "Perhaps you should suggest more names and I will decide if they are worthy."

Bee taps a finger on her chin, thinking. "Well, let me think. I don't think you're a Stan or a Bob and you're certainly not a Junior. You need a unique name that suits you, but also one I won't feel silly calling you." Her eyes go unfocused for a moment, and then she looks at me. "What about Victor? It might suit you."

Victor. As in, a champion. A winner. I like it. I nod. "Prime is good."

Her smile broadens. "I'll just have to remember to call you that. Victor. I think it's a good name." She gestures at my room. "Speaking of, what do you think of the improvements?"

I shrug.

She notices me leaning against the sink, and her expression becomes thoughtful. "You don't like the changes? Do you miss the cage? Is that it? Did you feel safer there?"

Safer? I snort. "I do not miss the cage, no."

"Then what is it, Victor?"

She is testing my name out, seeing if I like it. Seeing if I will respond to it. I like the sound of it, especially on her lips. Even so, the question she asks me is a little uncomfortable, because I hate showing weakness. Not that this shows weakness, but it shows I don't belong, which is almost as bad. "The bed," I point out, and then deliberately touch one of the spikes on my arms. "It won't work for me."

"Oh." Bee looks over at it, crestfallen. The mattress is a thin, soft pad, the blankets atop equally fragile. I'll shred them the moment I lie down, and then I know they will mock me, or take them away.

I don't want anyone snatching what's mine, even if it's a blanket I cannot use.

The human gets to her feet and moves to the bed, frowning. She picks up the blanket and folds it, moving to the foot of the mattress pad. "There are sturdier blankets," she offers. "I could switch them out. Perhaps a mattress filled with hay might be more efficient than one filled with cotton down?"

"Leave it alone," I growl. "I didn't suggest it because I want you to remove it. It's mine."

Bee smiles up at me, her managing smile, and she doesn't back off at the sound of my growl. She moves to my side and touches my arm, her fingers light on the short fur that covers my skin.

My body grows hot at that small touch, my cock instantly responding. "Wh-what are you doing?"

"I'm looking at your spikes." She gently runs her hand along one of my biceps, and I want to pull my cock free and jerk it, her touch feels so good. "Do they not retract?"

"If they do, I do not know how," I admit.

"Oh," she breathes, the sound soft. "There's dried blood at the base of this one." Her gaze moves up my arm, to the next deadly, thick spike jutting from my skin. "This one, too." Her soft gaze moves to my harder one. "Are you in pain?"

I grunt. What is the answer to that? Is there not always some pain? "They itch."

"I'll bring you an ointment," Bee says with a little smile. "And maybe you'll learn how to retract them with time."

Staring down at the small human, I fight the urge to grab her. I don't know if I want to startle her, or simply remind her that I'm a monster. She doesn't seem to be aware of this fact. "You should be afraid of me."

Bee pretends to consider this, but her smile remains on her face. "Why?"

"I'm a monster."

"No," she corrects. "You were cloned from a monster and treated poorly when you were awoken. I suspect anyone would have lashed out if that was the case." She pats my arm, rubbing it lightly, and then moves away, back to her stool.

I don't want her to go. Not even across the room. But I say nothing, because I cannot show weakness. The guards in the hall watch her, their faces stuffed with her foods, and between smacks of their lips, they comment on how fearless she is. How Riffin is an idiot for letting her do this.

"Letting" her. I suspect no one "lets" Bee do anything she doesn't want to do, and the thought amuses me.

"So we need a new mattress for you," Bee says, ticking it off on one hand as she sits down again. "A sturdier blanket. Ointment for your spikes and your wrists. What about clothes? Do you need better ones?"

I glance down at the loose trou covering my legs. They are all I have, and while I would be just as comfortable naked, it's obvious from the layers that the other males wear—and the layers that Bee wears—that no one is naked. People wear clothes around other people. So I shrug.

Bee continues to study me. "What about a bath? Would you like one?"

"Are you offering to bathe me, Bee?"

Her eyes go wide and she makes a little sound that might be a protest. "I—me? No." She tucks a strand of hair behind her ear and flushes, dropping her gaze. "Nice try though, Victor."

I grin, because why shouldn't I ask? And my grin widens when I catch a faint—very faint—new scent in the air.

Arousal. Just a hint of it, but it's enough to let me know that I affect her as much as she affects me. Good.

7

BEE

 ictor seems to be finding his footing. With a new name and the horrid cage out of his room, he stands a little straighter, his posture less bestial and more upright. Prouder. It's a good sign, and I'm happy for him. I want him to feel good about who he is, while accepting that he's not the monster everyone has him pegged to be. He's going to prove them all wrong and I'm going to be there every step of the way.

Well, maybe not every step of the way. I'm not going to bathe him.

Just thinking about the fact that he asked makes me flustered.

I know this is all a game to him. That even though his cage is gone, he's still a prisoner. Like any prisoner, he's going to test the bars to see where they give, or if they give at all. And I'm part of that cage, so of course he's going to test me.

I definitely should not find it exciting. It's fucked up that I do. It's even more fucked up that I look forward to him pushing at me, to see which of us will give first. I'm not used to men pushing back. Ever since I've been "freed," I've adopted a manipulative personality to protect myself. I act sugary sweet, like the Southern belles of old (even though I'm not southern) simply because I can get what I want that way. I stay safer if everyone knows and likes me, if they think of me fondly. It's the only weapon I have against a shitty universe that's determined to break me into pieces, so I wield it indiscriminately.

It's one reason I think I become frustrated with Riffin. He means well, but he always lets me have the upper hand, in exchange for kisses. Maybe it's fucked up that I find the fact that I can manipulate him like everyone else a little...repulsive.

Crulden—excuse me, Victor—sees through my bullshit. And even though it makes me a bit more vulnerable, it also makes me feel oddly *seen*. Like he knows it's all part of my survival instinct and sees the real me through it. It feels like he understands what it's like to have to put on a front to protect yourself around others. I wonder if that's why I'm drawn to him.

Either that or it is really long past time for me to break it off with Riffin.

I immediately drop the bathing conversation, because no good can come of that. Instead, I focus on something that can help him fit in with the rest of society—his eating habits. Victor eats like it's all about to be snatched away from him. He shoves his muzzle into his bowl and eats rapidly, flinging crumbs with such abandonment that it's a wonder he gets any of the food into his mouth. Today, I hand him a pair of the eating sticks that everyone here uses and a bowl full of noodles. The eating sticks aren't quite like chopsticks—they're fatter at one end than the other and the ends are flattened, so they're almost like tweezers. I got quickly used to them, but I know some humans still prefer forks and spoons. If Victor is going to mix in with everyone else, though, he needs to blend.

So, sticks it is.

I have the guards bring in a small table and another stool, and we sit across from each other as he practices. His big hands don't work well with the delicate utensils, and between that and the sloppiness of noodles, it's a lesson that doesn't go particularly well. We end up spending all afternoon fighting over how he needs to hold the sticks, getting him to cup the bowl properly instead of just shoving his face into the contents. I keep my smile on and my attitude bright, even when Victor gets all snarly and angry at me because I won't let him eat the now-cold soup without using the sticks.

We bicker over it for so long that I'm certain Victor is starting fights just to prick at me and get under my skin. I refuse to let him get to me, though. I stay strong and correct his grip and make him repeat the small motions over and over again.

"You are trying my patience, female," he growls, finally flinging the sticks into the bowl and shoving it aside.

"My name is Bee," I correct sweetly, plucking the sticks back out of the bowl and offering them to him again. "Not female. Not human. Bee. And you have to practice, Victor, or else you're never going to get anywhere. You need to show them that you're just the same as any other alien on this planet, and the first step is copying their mannerisms. So if you want to be a sulky baby, go right ahead, but if you want to beat them at their own game, you learn to use their tools."

And I wiggle the sticks at him.

His eyes narrow and he snatches them back out of my grip. Instead of flinging them to the floor as I expect, he clamps his jaw, glares at me, and holds them properly once more. Or tries to—his fingers are thick and his claws get in the way. But it's a close approximation.

I beam at him. "Now—"

The lights go out. The low, constant hum of power in the background whines and goes silent. Everything is creepily quiet and dark, and I stare at Victor. His eyes shine in the darkness, like a cat's.

I swallow hard, getting to my feet. "Is there a storm?"

The door to Victor's cell clicks, the electronic mechanism unlatching. The sound is overloud in the shadowy darkness.

Victor rises to his feet, turning toward the door. The very *unlocked* door that is no longer powered by the security grid in Lord va'Rin's estate.

Oh no, this is a bad idea. If he escapes, they'll kill him for sure.

I immediately fling myself against him. "Don't you even think about it."

He puts his hands on my arms, holding me against him. "Think about what?"

Double oh-no. He's using that low, sly purr that tells me he knows exactly what I'm asking and is fishing for my reaction. "Don't even think about escaping," I tell him. "We both know you're thinking it."

"Am I?" I could swear his thumb moves against my sleeve, the claw dragging over the material.

I stare up at him, his face cast in shadows except for those bright, glowing eyes. "You've wanted freedom since day one," I point out. "Don't play dumb. And think about it, Victor." I reach up and squeeze his lower arm, cutting my finger on one of the spikes. "Let's say this is a freak storm that knocked the power out. What then? Where do you go? You have no money, no shoes, no identification. Everyone's terrified of your appearance because you look like the rotten guy. They'll hunt you like a dog for the rest of your days, and that's the best-case scenario. Worst-case scenario, this is a trap and someone's hoping you rush through that door so they have a good excuse to shoot you."

Victor gazes down at me and then slowly nods. "You make an excellent point."

To my surprise, he doesn't let me go. Instead, he continues to grip my arms and steers me toward the corner of his room, where it's darkest, the light from the hall not penetrating the farthest corner. My heart hammers, and I should be afraid, but what I'm feeling isn't...fear? It's curiosity. He parks me against the wall, my back to the cool metal, and then immediately looms over me, bracing his big hands on the wall just above my shoulders.

And he gazes down at me.

I prickle with awareness. I can't see a thing because his big body is blocking out the light. All I can make out are his glowing eyes that are focused totally on me. Licking my lips, I gaze up at him and try to remain calm. "What's this all about?"

"Like you said. It could be a trap." His voice is velvety and smooth in the darkness, and oddly comforting. "So I'm protecting you."

"Me?" I sputter with amusement. "No one would set a trap for me."

"Wouldn't they?" He leans in, and I should be terrified to be stuck in the dark with a big, looming alien, but I'm mostly just relieved that he's not going to make a break for it. "Humans are prizes, remember? I might not know a lot of things, but I know that."

Mm, well, he's not completely wrong there. Even so, on a planet full of human captives, I'm not the most enticing pick, so I'm sure no one would go to such lengths to steal me, especially not out from under Lord va'Rin's nose. I reach up and pat his forearm and then duck under him to look out at the hall. It occurs to me that the guards didn't come in to protect me the moment the power was off. I don't know if that's kinda sad or if I should have expected it.

Unless Victor is right and I'm in danger. Just the thought makes me humph. Humans are prizes, indeed. "More like a booby prize. Trust me, no one really wants a human for a pet.

We're messy and stubborn, we don't respond well to training, and we make messes all over the floors. We have very particular diets, too. The last thing you want is a gassy human pet at the foot of your bed."

"Is that where your master kept you?" Victor asks. "At the foot of his bed?"

"I don't recall giving you permission to ask about that," I say lightly, and pretend to gaze up at the ceiling. Not that I can see it, since, darkness. "I wonder how long the power will be out for?"

"No questions about the past," he muses. "I understand. I expect if I had an unpleasant one, I wouldn't wish to talk about it, either. The memories I do have are grisly, but they're filled with pleasure, at least. Even the ones full of pain are still edged with pleasure. I think Crulden liked being physically hurt."

I wrinkle my nose at the thought. "And you have those memories?"

"Some of them, but they're hazy." Victor grunts, his big body still protecting mine from nothing at all. "I have memories of some fights, too. All of them wins. Either I never lost or I chose not to remember those."

"That wasn't you," I point out again. "You're a clone, remember, Victor. That's why we're giving you a new name. And probably a bath." Now that I'm caged under his arms, his scent is everywhere. It should be unpleasant, but I actually don't mind it. He smells sweaty, of course, but that's to be expected. It's not a bad sweaty, though. Just...sweaty.

I peek under his arm at the hall again, but I don't see anything out there. It's just darkness. If the two guardsmen that are supposed to be protecting me are out there, they're not exactly rushing to save me. I'm pretty sure they're not even trying. So much for upgrading their weapons. I wonder if Victor's collar is offline, too.

"Even if it wasn't me, it's good to remember those bouts."

"Is it? Why?"

I could swear he grins in the darkness, even though I can only make out the outline of his face. It's the way his tusks move, I suppose. I should be horrified, but I'm intrigued. I'm not as disgusted by his face as I once was. It's different—plenty different—but at the end of the day, he's just another alien and I probably look strange to him, too.

"Because it reminds me how good it feels to win," he rasps. When I stiffen with alarm, he continues, as if he can smell my fear. "Not the violence itself. Just...the knowledge that I've won. That I've been the best. And that I've got a prize—however small—waiting for me."

"And that motivates you?" I ask politely, because I'm sure some of those prizes in the past were people like me. "A prize at the end of the fight? Is that why you're staying here instead of running?"

"I'm staying here because I'm protecting you." Victor's voice is that husky growl again, and it makes my stomach flip. Not out of fear...out of something unnameable. "But since you mention motivation...remember when you first arrived? And you asked me what I wanted for incentive to work with you?"

I remember that conversation very well. For some reason, though, my body is heating up the longer he keeps whispering to me. Maybe he's giving off a lot of body heat. I wonder if it'd be obvious of me if I started fanning my face. "Did you decide what you want as your prize?"

"I did." Victor leans down. "You can steal my breath like you do your boyfriend."

Steal his breath...? "You mean kissing?"

"Is that what it's called? When he shoves his tongue in your mouth and licks you? When he puts his lips over yours?"

I swallow hard, because I'm not sure what to think of this. Victor wants me to kiss him? It's a terrible idea. Not only would it destroy any boundaries we have between us, but I find his tusks and sharp teeth more than a little alarming. What if kissing him is repulsive? It would hurt his feelings and destroy anything we've built up if I'm disgusted by him. "I don't want to do that, Victor."

He laughs, and the sound isn't angry at all, which makes me relax a little. "Why is that, little Bee? Because you're not attracted to me? I know what I look like. I don't expect a human to see what I've got to offer and salivate over it. But you know what I realized? You're not attracted to that fool you call your boyfriend, and you kiss him. So I figure it doesn't matter."

I make a sound of protest. "It's very rude of you to point out that sort of thing, Victor."

"How is it rude? Because it's the truth and you don't want to admit it?"

I hate that he chuckles. I hate that he finds all of this amusing. If Riffin knew I was inside Crulden's—Victor's—cell right now with the power off and he was hovering over me, he'd lose his mind with worry. Actually, I'm not sure if it'd be worry as much as he'd be upset that another male was pissing all over his territory, which just fills me with even more disgust for my situation. "Kissing Riffin is different," I point out. "It's not the same."

"I know it's not the same," Victor continues in that reasonable tone. "It's not the same because when he kisses you, you feel nothing. But when I kiss you, you won't." He leans in, his voice a mere whisper. "We both know I could make you come."

I gasp, the sound breathless and turned on despite myself. I can't believe he's bringing this up again. "You hush."

Victor just leans closer, his voice floating around me in the darkness. "He doesn't care that you're not aroused, little Bee. To him, your mouth is just him claiming you to show off to others. He's not interested in your pleasure. But see, I have a lot of time to think in this cell of mine. I think about you. And I think about how I'd react in that situation. Would I shove my tongue deep into your mouth for my pleasure alone? Would I steal your breath and not care that you were only tolerating my touch? That your cunt remained dry as bone no matter how much I put my mouth on you?" His voice dips. "But see, I like winning."

"Winning?" I echo, practically panting in the darkness.

"Mmmhmm. And if you don't feel pleasure when I touch you, then it's not a prize. See, it's not about me. It's about tasting you. It's about licking that sweet mouth of yours and gauging your response."

My breasts tighten against my clothes, my nipples aching. I say nothing, because I don't trust my voice. Not any longer.

"I'd change what I was doing," he continues silkily, "until I figured out what you liked. And I'd keep doing that, because I want your cunt juicy and wet with need, Bee. I'd need that. I want that scent in my nose so I know that when I kiss you, you're in there with me, and you want my mouth as badly as I want to give it to you." Victor shifts, and I feel one claw skim along the line of my jaw. "And that's the difference between me and that fool you kiss. I'd make you come. I'd make you wet with need. And that scares you, doesn't it?"

I clear my throat and manage a stern, "Of course not."

"Little liar." His thumb strokes my cheek. "But like I said, it doesn't matter. You kiss him and you don't want it. So if you want me to keep cooperating so you can keep this job of yours, you'll kiss me, too."

"That's blackmail," I breathe, both horrified and titillated.

"Don't care. Do we have an agreement?"

Before I can answer, the lights come back on.

8

VICTOR

The lights return, the door lock clicks into place, and my collar hums as it comes online again, shivering at my throat to remind me of its presence.

Bee pulls away, startled and breathless. I can tell by the look on her face that she wasn't expecting my request. She needs time to think about it. That's fine. I've got nothing but time. What's interesting to me is that the more that I pushed for her to kiss me, the more aroused her scent grew. She protests at the thought of being coerced into putting her mouth on mine...but she's still interested. She was more aroused from my suggestion than she's ever been from her so-called boyfriend and his mouth touching hers.

Before I can say anything, the shock-collar lights up, tightening around my throat and sending a harsh surge of energy through my system. I remember to pretend to be affected, and stagger backward, making choking noises as I do.

"Crulden?" Bee gasps, reaching for me. "Victor?"

I don't answer, closing my eyes and pretending to be lost in the pain of the shock-collar. I'm secretly pleased at her distress, though. She's worried about me, though she doesn't need to be. It's still nice to see.

"Female," one of the guards calls through the window. "Come away from him! Come to the door. You're free!"

She makes an exasperated noise in her throat, reaching out and touching my hand. The shock travels through her system and she yelps, quickly drawing back. "You're hurting him! Stop!"

"The power is back on," the guards call, frantic. "You can escape now!"

"I'm not IN any danger," she bellows back, and then mutters under her breath. "Oaf." I hear her steps move away from me, and the door buzzes as she opens it and steps outside. "Are you shocking him? Turn it off!"

"Are you hurt?" they ask, clearly worried for the female who'd been trapped with a monster like me for all of a few moments.

Bee's irritation is clear. "Of course I'm not hurt. He won't hurt me. He's trying very hard and you're not supporting him, you know. Turning on the shock-collar the moment you feel in control is a terrible, cowardly thing to do."

"But—"

"Turn it off right now," Bee demands. Her voice is no longer delicate or sweet. It is furious, and I'm impressed that she's let her facade slip to defend me. "Turn it off right now or we're going to have to talk about how Crulden was the only one that thought about *my* safety when the power went off. Because I didn't see you two rushing in there. Do I need to point this out to your supervisors? Or are we understanding each other clearly now?"

The collar turns off, the buzzing ceasing. Even though it's not enough to truly affect me, it's annoying and I'm glad it's gone. I rub my throat, opening my eyes to glare at the two useless guards. Bee's hands are on her hips, and she's glaring at them equally.

I find this...charmingly adorable.

AFTER BEE LEAVES for the day and I'm alone in my cell, the guards flick the lights off. "Night night, Crulden," one calls, and the other laughs.

I don't mind. The darkness doesn't bother me. It lets me think. I have a great many things to think about today.

I sort through my memories—or rather, Crulden's memories. It doesn't bother me that I've been cloned from him. That I've got no memories except his remnants and whatever's been implanted in my mind. The more I sort through his memories and feelings, the less they feel like mine. Those brutal arena fights? The feeling of ripping someone's spine out through their back? Those are someone else's joys. There's an old, ugly memory of a female—something with green skin and big, sad eyes—shrieking in terror as Crulden stalks towards her in the arena, but I don't dig deeper.

The one that I'm cloned from might have wanted to hurt females, but I don't. It's not a fair fight. They're not even competing.

I think of Bee, instead of delving deeper into those memories. I think of the intoxicating scent of her arousal. I scented it for the first time today, and I already know I need more of it. I think about that scent and what her cunt would feel like if I got to touch her. Would she be as soft there, between her thighs? As plump and touchable as everywhere else? Or is the texture different? I search through my spotty memories, but I come to no answer for this. I imagine her smooth and sweet, then, a dusky pink like her mouth. I imagine droplets of her arousal sliding down her rounded thighs as she crosses her legs, and my cock aches with so much need that it sets me on edge. The cot will be destroyed if I use it, so I grab the blanket from the end of the bed and move to the darkest, most shadowy corner in my room and sink to the floor. I haul the blanket over my front, sitting with my back to the wall and my knees up.

And I slide a hand to my cock.

It aches. It's ached for hours now, ever since Bee's scent first drifted into my nose.

I free my cock from my trou and grip it tight. I'm not entirely sure of the motions, but instinct compels me to work the shaft with quick, fast motions. I imagine Bee's scent, and then I imagine Bee under me, her eyes soft, her mouth open as she breathes my new name. *Victor. Victor.* I squeeze and jerk until the need comes to a head and explodes out of me. With a muffled gasp, I soak the blanket with the wash of my release, and coat my hand, too. I wipe myself clean on a corner of the blanket and then move to the sink to wash off. As I do, I smell blood.

My palm is ripped open, destroyed from the barbs that cover my shaft. I'd barely felt them as I worked my cock, but I feel the sting now. Worse than that, I think of Bee. I think of pushing my barb-covered cock into her soft body and how she would cry out in pain.

My cock shrivels at the thought. Why do I bother even fantasizing? Even if Bee wanted to be mine, I could not have her. She is a soft, fragile alien, a human. And I am a splice with claws and spikes and a barbed cock. I am not meant for soft things.

It's a disappointing thought. I clench my fist, watching the blood rivulets cascade down my hand, and wish I'd been cloned from anyone else.

Someone that could touch Bee.

9

BEE

I don't see Riffin for days. At first I think it's just because his schedule changed, but when more time passes, I suspect he's avoiding me.

The guardsmen are terrible gossips. I wonder if any of them told Riffin that I'd been going into Victor's cell and that we talk for long periods of time? That when we speak, it's usually in low voices so we can't be overheard? That he makes me laugh with his sly comments and when the power went out, he protected me with his body?

I wonder if Riffin suspects something between us. The thought makes me squirm on my stool, as I sit, watching Victor fold his new blankets over the thick, hay-filled mattress on his bed. I should be paying attention to his movements—the bed-making is a basic skill as well as a test in patience and teaching him to be careful with his claws—but I'm distracted. Terribly distracted. I keep wondering if I should back off in regard to

Victor. I've proved my point—that I can be patient and work with those that are difficult. I've made progress with him, and even if he showed signs of violence, I think he's come far enough that no one's going to "dispose" of him without asking questions. It'd be the perfect time for me to re-petition First Rank Novis about getting my job as Port's social worker and hand Victor off to someone else.

But I...can't.

He tries so hard not to show emotion, but when I arrive for the day, it's like he lights up from within. His eyes get a sparkle in them, and his tail flicks at the sight of me. I wouldn't say that he smiles—with his sharp teeth and those nasty, wicked-looking tusks, it's more of a snarl—but I've learned to recognize when he's pleased.

And honestly, seeing him is the best part of my day, too. I've been noticing which foods he merely eats, and which foods he relishes. I've noticed when his gaze falls on my figure if I wear a particularly attractive outfit. I wear my hair up because I catch him gazing at my ear, or my neck, and it makes me shiver.

He wants me to kiss him if he continues "behaving." Victor hasn't brought it up again, because there hasn't been a moment alone, but it's lingering in the back of my mind every day. Every time I see him, I wonder if this will be the day that he asks again. If this will be the day I have to give an answer.

I keep telling myself I don't know what my answer would be, but I'm also lying to myself.

Because I keep showing up every day. And at night, I wonder what it'd be like to kiss him. I touch my mouth and wonder how it'd feel against his tusks or his hard, uncomfort-able-looking mouth that is stretched over those tusks and never quite closes properly. I wonder what it'd be like to have one of those big, clawed hands brushing over my skin, touching me.

I almost touch myself, too.

I'm not quite there yet. Sex has felt "off limits" ever since I was stolen from Earth and made to serve in an alien's bed. It was a year of hell, and when I was freed, I found that all desire for any kind of intimacy had burned away. I felt like a pot that had been left to boil down on the stove, and all that remained was the charred residue. I was fine with never being touched again. Ever. It was enough to be free and to realize that I never had to have another man in my life.

If nothing else, Victor and his promise to kiss me have taught me that I'm not completely dead inside.

I should really think about how I'm going to move forward with Riffin—or if that's going to happen at all—but I can't seem to focus. Instead, I keep my dreamy gaze on Victor's big form, the annoyed twitch of his tail as I make him do hospital corners on his lumpy bed. I find that tail increasingly fascinating. There's a gap in the back of his pants—his trou, as they call it here—that allows for the tail, and beyond that, you can see just a hint of skin. In the case of Victor, it's that light, fuzzy fur that covers his body. I wonder if he's soft. I wonder...

Victor straightens, his tail flicking madly. He turns to look at me, and his eyes are hooded, the front of his trou tight. The fabric there is tented, and he takes in a deep breath as he looks at me. "Done."

I get to my feet, a little flustered. "Perfect, thank you," I chirp automatically, sinking back into my cheery persona. As I move to inspect the bed, Victor doesn't move. I deliberately step closer to him, and I could swear I hear him sniff. Oh mercy, am I aroused again? Is that what's making him react? I swallow hard.

After he'd propositioned me, I'd returned home that night to find my panties soaked. I realized that Victor must have smelled it, and that probably only encouraged him. I should be embarrassed, or angry that he can tell my emotions by a scent. Instead, it makes my pulse flutter, and I suspect other parts of me flutter, too. It's going to be another soaked panty day when I get home.

Which means the best thing I can do is ignore it. So I move to the bed, touching the thicker, sturdy material of the plas-blanket, and frown when I notice a dark, wet bead of liquid on the material. "What's this?"

"Nothing," Victor says, voice tight. "Is my lesson done now?"

I touch the droplet, and it's warm and deep red against my finger. "Are you bleeding?" I ask, horrified. "Victor, are you hurt?"

His nostrils flare, jaw clenching, and he looks as if he'd like to punch the wall. "It's nothing, Bee."

"It's not nothing to me. Where are you hurt?" Fury rises in my chest, hot and urgent. "Did someone hurt you? Did they come in here with more shock-sticks? Or more collars?" I'm realizing just how vulnerable Victor is. He's agreed to the collar and to go along with things, but the others haven't exactly agreed to play nice. They could be perfect dicks—like First Rank Novis was to Victor when he first awoke—and would receive nothing more than a slap on the wrist from Lord va'Rin.

Heck, they'd probably get a raise from their commander.

I shake a finger at Victor, trembling with anger. "If you don't tell me, I'm going to march right into Lord va'Rin's personal rooms and—"

Victor growls. It's a low, irritated sound, but I'm not afraid. If anything, it makes me want to growl right back at him. Before I can snap a response, he extends his hands, palms up. They're shredded, with myriad scratches marring the surface, along with a few deeper gouges. They look as if they've gone through a cheese grater.

"Oh my god, what happened?" I take his hands carefully in mine, examining them. I'm shocked at the damage, and I'm upset that this happened right under my nose. "What is this,

Victor? Are the guards torturing you?" I look up at him, horrified. "Talk to me."

"It's nothing," he growls again. "Leave me alone, Bee."

"Not until you tell me who did this! Victor—"

He leans into my face, his expression furious. "I did this, all right?"

"You?" I squeak, surprised. "What—"

Victor opens his mouth, and then jerks backward, reaching for the collar at his neck. Helpless, I look over at the observation window, and sure enough, one of the guards is frowning, his hand on the control panel. He must have seen Victor get in my face and assumed the worst. "Turn it off," I call. "It's just a misunderstanding!"

The guard frowns at me but does as I ask. Victor grunts, and I know the collar's been shut off again. He glares at the window but stalks away from me, as if he doesn't want to talk.

My heart is breaking in my chest. I don't understand. Why is Victor self-harming? Is it because he's bored? Restless? Miserable in this cage? I've got to fix it. I don't want him hurting himself. "Talk to me," I whisper, taking a step toward him. "Please tell me what's troubling you, Victor. Aren't we friends?"

He doesn't answer me, and I suspect I know why. It's that "friends" word. He's not interested in being my friend. He's made it clear that he wants to kiss me. He wants to experiment with me. He wants to test out his sexuality with me. And...I want that, too.

"Come on," I say when he remains quiet. "Let me take care of you." I gently take his wrist in my grasp, and when he doesn't pull away, I tug, indicating I want to bring him to the sink. He reluctantly lets me lead him, and I park him next to the sink and indicate he should stay, then I grab the stool from our table and drag it over. I want to chide him for not telling me about his wounds, but if he's self-harming, of course he's going to hide it. He's not going to declare it to me.

It makes me want to cry, but I can't be weak. I need to be strong in the best way I know how. So I put on my Happy Bee smile, wait for him to sit down, and then I get to work cleaning his wounds. "We'll get these fixed up for you," I tell him in a chipper voice. "It's a good thing we have that ointment I brought the other day."

Victor just grunts.

That's fine. I don't need an answer. Perkily, I tell him all about the time I raced my bike as a schoolgirl and collided with the neighbor's garbage can. "They had a rock garden, too. It was the worst place for me to fall, so of course I fell there." I chuckle. "I had skinned knees for weeks, and my mother used a cleaner called Betadine that makes the wound this bright, ugly, orangey red. It was very distressing for me as a child, because I liked to wear pretty dresses and put bows in my hair. From the knee up, I was adorable. From the knee down, I was an orange-red, skinned mess." I smile at him as I dab the ointment on the cuts. I don't know what made them, but I'm going to guess that it has something to do with his claws. Maybe someday he'll feel enough trust to tell me what he did and why. "If you'll wait here, I'll get some bandages from the med center—"

"Stay." The word is low and warm. He looks at me, and with him seated, we're practically the same height. "Please."

"Oh." I'm a sucker for a good "please." "All right, then." I look around for something I can use as a makeshift bandage. I don't see anything, though, so I improvise. I hold out the long hem of my tunic—it's a basic blue tunic with a flaring skirt that goes to my knees and is belted at the waist over leggings. Mine is faded, since it's a hand-me-down from another woman, but the material is soft and absorbent. I gesture at the hem, approximating a three-inch section. "Can you use your claws to cut this here, to here?"

Victor shakes his head. "I don't want to ruin your clothing."

"Then let me go get bandages for you from the med center," I chirp. "I'm happy with either."

He hesitates and then sinks a claw into the material, tearing it. I glance over at the guards in the window, giving them a chipper thumbs up so they don't panic. "At least this way, I'll smell like you," Victor murmurs. "I'll sniff my hands all day long."

Oh my god.

That simple, quiet statement should not make my body flood with awareness. Heat throbs between my thighs as he finishes ripping the bottom off my tunic, and I turn slowly in place so it'll tear evenly. I keep thinking about his words, the only sound between us the steady tear of the fabric.

I'll sniff my hands all day long.

Biting my lip, I take the length from him, tear it in half again lengthwise, and then take the first strip and begin to carefully wrap it around his wounded hand. "I hope this feels better," I whisper. "Now that they're taken care of."

"Bee," Victor says my name so low I wonder if I'm imagining it. "I can smell your arousal."

More heat spreads through my body. I ignore it, attentively wrapping his hands. "I know."

"I love the smell of it," he growls. "Love it."

I suck in a breath, both charmed and overwhelmed at his statement. "I know."

Victor watches me with intense eyes. "I'm the only one you get wet for. Me and me alone."

I don't answer that. It feels like too much. I finish wrapping the one hand and then focus on the other. He stays still, letting me tend to him, and when I'm done, I run my thumb over the palm, making sure it's covered and no ointment seeps out. His claws are angled toward the ceiling, toward my face with his hand turned like this, but I'm not afraid in the slightest. I'm more worried he'll hurt himself again. Like there's too much boiling over inside him without an outlet.

I glance over at the guards in the hall, but they're not paying attention to us. They're talking about something, munching on the cookies I brought. So I decide to be a little bold. I lift Victor's hand higher and kiss the tip of his thumb, letting my lips skate over it. "Promise me you won't hurt yourself tonight," I whisper. "I can't bear it."

"I promise," he says, and devours me with his eyes.

10

BEE

*A*fter I leave Victor's quarters for the night, I pick up the now-empty cookie plate and pause. Should I say something to the guards? Make sure that they watch him closely? They're terrible guards, young men who don't pay attention to anything except idle chatter. I can't be angry, though, because it suits my purposes. I like that they're wretched at their job, because it gives me quiet time with Victor.

I decide not to say anything at all, because it'll feel like a betrayal if I do.

I decide instead to go straight to Lord va'Rin.

Even though I'm not invited, I take the long walk towards the large estate. The garrison compound is tucked between a few rolling hills and is maybe a fifteen-minute walk away from the actual estate. If we were back home, I'd say it was a few blocks, but there's no blocks here, just pastoral fields, fencing to denote property, and the occasional air-sled zipping overhead. I head straight for the main entrance of the large estate. There are several guards strategically placed around the decorative walls that surround the house and gardens, but since I know most of them, they just nod at me when I arrive and let me pass. The estate is massive. I haven't seen a lot of trees on Risda III—it's mostly rolling hills and plains in this part of the world —but there are several pretty varieties that frame the house, along with a few sculptures. Rock cobblestone walkways dance around the manicured lawns, and the exterior of the house itself looks like something out of a dream - space mansion meets old English castle. There are turrets on the four corners of the estate, which makes it seem a bit like a compound, but the windows and doors are all "space" modern. There's a distinct Earth-flavor to things, though, like the way that the lines of windows are tall, narrow points instead of squares, or the double doors that look as if they were shipped from Tudor England. It's like someone saw a picture of an Earth castle and said, "Let's make that on our end of space." Come to think of it, maybe that's exactly what happened, given that Lord va'Rin is known to dote on his human wife.

I march up to the door, determination in my step. I'm going to talk to Lord va'Rin about how Crulden—Victor—is self-harming and how we need to change his program, to show him more compassion. Maybe he's lonely and desperate and can't show it. Maybe there's something else going on. If we can't figure it out, maybe someone needs to stay with him at all times. I'll certainly volunteer. I raise my hand to knock—

The doors chime, and an access panel slides out of the wall to the side of the old-fashioned doors. "Please stand facing the doors so a retinal scan can be performed. When that is completed, state name and purpose of visit. Thank you."

"Oh, um, Bee Wilson, and my purpose is to talk to Lord va'Rin about—"

Before I can finish, the door opens and I take a step back in surprise. Riffin appears, a look of surprise on his face, wearing the livery uniform of Lord va'Rin's household guard. This must be his new assignment. Well...poop. Of all the timing. "Bee?"

"Wow, Riffin, hi. Small world."

He frowns at me, moving out to greet me on the doorstep. "I do not see what the size of the planet has to do with this situation, Bee. What are you doing here?"

Okay, well, I guess I can't get away from the situation. I resist the urge to wring my hands and instead put on my happiest, most efficient Bee-Gets-Shit-Done smile. "I'm here to discuss Victor's progress with Lord va'Rin."

"Victor?" he echoes blankly.

"The prisoner?"

His face immediately changes to a thunderous expression and he looks around angrily, as if to make sure no one else heard me. He shuts the door behind him and grabs my arm, hauling me off the elegant porch. "He's not a prisoner, Bee, and saying things like that is going to upset Lord va'Rin. He's doing his best to help that monster."

"But he's wearing a shock collar," I protest. "And he's not allowed to leave his room—"

"Would you let a creature like that loose in Port? Amidst all those helpless females?" Riffin hisses the words at me, clearly furious, and his fingers dig into my arm. "Be realistic, Bee."

I hate that his words make me feel guilty. Do I trust Victor in Port? Where so many of the women are damaged from their captivity and are afraid of aliens? I'm not sure of the answer. "He's not a creature. That's unfair."

Riffin shakes his head. "You should go home, Bee. You..." His face changes and he sniffs the air, confused. A moment later, his eyes flare with anger and he shoves me away from him. "That *scent*."

"What scent?"

His nose twitches and he bares his teeth at me. "You're

aroused. By that monster?" His hand feels like a vise on my arm. "That filthy thing turns you on and yet I don't? Is that what you like? You want to be violated?" He flings me away from him, and I have to stagger to keep my balance. "Is that why you push me off, Bee? Because you're keffed in the head after what happened to you? Do you want me to be abusive to you? Will that turn you on?"

I back up, pressing against the wall, and I'm horrified at Riffin's anger. The things he's saying are awful, and yet I'm also kicking myself. I should have known that if I came here smelling like I was turned on, someone would notice it. I forget that the mesakkah—the blue, horned race of aliens that run the show—have sensitive noses. Maybe not as sensitive as Victor, but sensitive enough. The damage is done, though. I hadn't counted on running into Riffin, but maybe this is a blessing in disguise. "You're being unfair, Riffin. And it's time we talked about us anyhow."

"Us?" He laughs, the sound bitter as he paces back and forth. "I'm starting to think there is no 'us,' Bee. There's only me pushing you for things you clearly don't want." Riffin shakes his head, his horns glinting in the late afternoon sunlight. "I never thought I'd be competing with Crulden the Ruiner for my keffing female."

He makes it sound like I'm a prize to be won, and that's the nail in the coffin for me. "Maybe you should look at the reasons you want to be in this relationship with me," I point out. "It's certainly not because of who I am."

"Don't pretend you're the wounded party here, Bee." Riffin shakes his head again, then rakes a hand through his hair, mussing it. "Just...go home, all right? We'll pretend this never happened."

What the heck? Pretend this never happened? It's ugly and unpleasant, but in a way, it's a good thing. I'm sad to lose Riffin as a friend, but after what he's said just now, I don't think we can stay friends anyhow...much less dating. "I need to talk to Lord va'Rin first."

Riffin snorts. "Your timing is all wrong, then. He's off-planet with his wife."

Oh no. "He is? For how long?" When Riffin doesn't answer me, I change tactics, putting on my efficient smile. "All right, then. I'll go talk to First Rank Novis—"

"No, you won't."

If there's something I hate, it's a man telling me what to do. My back goes stiff and I straighten, lifting my chin. "Riffin, he's the one overseeing my job. I need to speak to him—"

"With your cunt reeking from wanting that creature?" Riffin snarls. He grabs my arm again and hauls me off the porch, pulling me down the pretty stone walkway of the estate and toward the gate. "No, you won't. You're going to go home and wash that stink off of you. You think First Rank Novis will appreciate that you get turned on by that thing? You value your job so much, act like it."

"Let go of me, Riffin," I say tightly, struggling against his arm. The other guards watch me curiously but don't help out as Riffin tugs me past them. They know we're a couple, and I guess in their eyes, this is just a tiff? It angers me, but I'm not surprised. For all that the aliens here talk a big game about letting this place be a safe haven for human women, they still view humans as slightly stupid things that need to be protected from themselves.

"Go home, Bee," Riffin says again, escorting/dragging me out of the estate. Once I'm past the fence, he gestures at the distant town of Port on the horizon. "Get an air-sled, go home, wash up, and we'll talk about this tomorrow."

I don't want to talk about this tomorrow. I'm not even sure I ever want to talk to Riffin ever again. But the guards are staring at us with surprise and interest, and I know they'll be gossiping about our fight before the night is out. So I straighten my tunic, lift my chin, and smile sweetly at the nearest guard. "Who wants to give me a ride back to Port?"

THE NEXT MORNING, I shower twice before I head to the garrison. I scrub my nether parts so hard that my skin burns, and I slather on the herbal paste that everyone here uses for deodorant. My arms are mottled from finger-sized bruises where Riffin grabbed me, so I put on a long-sleeved tunic even though it's warm today. The bruises make me sad because they feel like the end of something. I know Riffin was upset, and I made him upset. I also know he's much stronger than me and probably doesn't realize he hurt me, so I'm not mad over them.

But I'm also done with him. What he said wasn't acceptable, and yet at the same time, I needed to hear it.

I'm attracted to Victor, with his ugly, tusked mouth and his claws and spikes and his lion-like mane. Victor, with his feral, brutal attitude. And Riffin, with his politeness and eager-to-please attitude, is not doing anything for me. So it's time I cut the cord on that relationship. I'm sad, but I'm also relieved. Deep inside, I think I've always known it wasn't going anywhere. Maybe that was part of the appeal, too, that I could use Riffin as a boyfriend and thus keep all other men at bay.

I recognize that I'm a mess, and at least I can own it.

I tug my sleeves down my arms, making sure all the bruises are hidden, and head to the kitchen to pick up the baked goods I stayed up late last night making. As I do, I run into Melanie. She gives me a bright-eyed look and practically bounces over to me. "Oh my god, Bee, guess what! I got my farm! They told me it's ready and all I have to do is establish ownership with the Port custodians and I'll be good to go."

"That's wonderful." I smile at Melanie. I know she's been waiting patiently for her farm for a few weeks now. Lord va'Rin's people have been busy and I know she's been antsy. Normally I'd be jealous that another woman is moving out of the boarding house and away to her new life, but today my thoughts are full of Victor. "I'll miss seeing you. Will you write me?"

Melanie giggles and flings herself at me for a hug. She's the only person I've met that's more buoyant than me, personality-wise. "Of course I will! And you know I'll be back in Port all the time."

I'm not sure if she realizes how time-consuming farming can be. I had mine for all of a week before I developed my allergy, and I was intensely grateful for it. I'm most definitely not a farmer. "Just remember to ask for help if you need it."

"Oh, Bee." Melanie smiles, giving me another exuberant hug. "It's farming. How hard can it be?"

Poor, sweet Melanie has no idea what she's getting into. I just hug her back, pat her shoulder and tell her how happy I am for her. Maybe I'm wrong and she'll be a natural. Maybe she'll excel at farming and find that it gives her life meaning. I hope so. I want her to be happy. She deserves it.

Just like Victor does.

Wow, I've really got him on the brain today. I can feel myself blushing as I pick up the pan of waffles (my go-to when I don't have a lot of time to bake) and murmur excuses to Melanie about how I'm going to be late for work.

WHEN I GET to the garrison, something immediately feels wrong. The guards posted don't look me in the eye as I go in, and they don't seem excited about the food that I've brought, whereas normally the sight of me with breakfast brings all kinds of enthusiastic commentary. It makes me wonder if they've heard about the fight I had with Riffin, or if he's complained about me to the others. Surely he wouldn't tell everyone in the garrison that I'm attracted to Victor and not him? I can't help but wonder, however, because the mood is downright strange.

It grows even stranger as I go inside, and the hall outside of Victor's quarters is full of guards. There's at least six of them, armed with the stun guns, watching him through the window. They barely glance at me as I arrive.

My heart plummets at the sight. Immediately, I know something's wrong with Victor. I dump the package of waffles onto the snack table set at the far end of the hall and race back to the reinforced windows that allow the guards to watch Victor's movements from the safety of the hall.

Except...Victor isn't moving. His back is to us, his spiky, terrifying-looking shoulders hunched. He crouches low in the center of the room, and there are massive scratches up and down the walls, everywhere I look, as if he was clawing to get free. There are even furrows ripped into the floor, and as I stare in shock, his hands go down to the tile once more. He digs his claws into the floor and drags them, making a god-awful sound and tearing fresh furrows into the marble tile.

"What happened?" I breathe, horrified. Something's happened to make him regress like this, and I don't know what it is. Last night when I left, we were fine. He was good. He was even...teasing me. Flirting with me in that strange way of his. The feral man I see before me is very, very far from fine. "What's going on?"

The guard closest to me—Kennak—shakes his head, stepping protectively in front of me when I try to approach the window to get a better look. "You shouldn't be in here." He nods to another. "Robas, take her out of here."

When Robas steps forward, I sidestep his helping hand and move to the far side of Kennak. "Tell me what happened. What triggered him? What caused this?" And is it related to the self-harming he was doing yesterday? My stomach ties in knots. Should I have said something to the guards? It would have felt like a violation of Victor's trust, but maybe it could have prevented this. "He was fine when I left yesterday. Something happened."

Kennak shakes his head, neatly positioning himself so I can't get to the door panel. "It started last night, a few hours after dusk. He was fine one moment, laying on his bed, and in the next, he jumped up and started pacing. He wouldn't talk to us when we attempted to communicate, and when he started clawing at the walls, we made the choice to tranquilize him. The moment he awoke, he started doing this again, though." He rubs his jaw, thinking. "We might have to take drastic measures if he presents a threat to others."

Oh god. I can only imagine what those "drastic measures" are. They want to kill him. They think he's unsafe. That his presence is a threat to the settlers here. As I watch Victor claw runnels into the tile, I can't even say that they're wrong. He can't be around anyone like this.

Even so, I can't give up on him.

Up until yesterday, I really thought I was getting through to him. I thought I was making a difference.

"Female," Kennak says in a gentle voice. "Perhaps you should return home this day. There is nothing for you to do here."

I shake my head. "I can help him," I promise in my normal perky voice, even if I feel like I'm dying a bit inside. Seeing Victor regress like this is absolutely crushing my soul. It hurts that I can't help him. It hurts that he's clearly struggling and there's nothing I can do. "Please, let me help him."

"How?" Kennak's grip tightens on his weapon. "You're not going in there today. Not today, maybe not ever again."

Never again? The thought is painful. No more conversations with Victor. No more teasing lessons that end with that belly-fluttering tension. No more of him curling those claws against his thigh, as if he wants to reach out and touch me but doesn't trust himself. No more of him watching me like I'm a particularly delicious morsel he can't wait to eat. "I can help him," I say, keeping my tone bright. "He likes the food I bring, right? Maybe that'll help shake him out of this spell."

"No," Kennak begins.

I ignore him and push my way toward the window, but I don't reach for the panel. Instead, I knock on the impenetrable glass, glass that I've been told is strong enough to withstand tons of force. "Victor," I call out, even though he probably can't hear me through the walls. "Victor, it's me, Bee. You have to stop this."

I don't expect my plea to do anything. It's just me desperately hoping for something to change. This can't be the way Victor goes out. To my surprise, though, his shoulders tense. His tail flicks, and his head lowers. "Bee," he growls, and it's just enough of an enunciation of my name to realize that he's not growling. He's responding.

My heart flares with hope. I clutch Kennak's arm. "Did you hear that? He's calling for me."

"Female," Kennak warns with a look. "I don't know what you think you heard, but this is a bad idea."

"He responded," I repeat stubbornly. "Let me go in there and talk to him. I can make him stop this."

"You're insane. I'm not letting you keffing anywhere near that door. First Rank Novis will have my head if he tries anything." Kennak tries to pull me away. "I'm not about to let a human female get murdered by that beast on my watch."

I twist out of his grip, ignoring the pain from the bruises that go up my arm. I don't know what's going on but it's clear to me that Victor needs me. He needs my help, and I'm going to go to him. I glance up at Kennak, who has, by all accounts, been as pleasant as expected. He doesn't like Victor, but he's a stickler for the rules and is one of the more watchful guards. I need to use that dedication to his job against him. "Lord va'Rin wants him reformed, not murdered," I say reasonably. "I know you're worried about the safety of the guards here, but I assure you, I can fix this. Let me go in and talk to him."

"No."

I bite a fingernail and do my best to look helpless and girly. "It's just...how are we going to tell Lord va'Rin when he returns to find Victor dead that we didn't do everything possible to help him? That we took the easy way out? That we didn't try every avenue? He'll be so very disappointed. And think of the message it sends to the other rescued gladiators." I gaze up at him with a beseeching look. "We know Victor won't harm me. Even when he's been upset with the guards, he hasn't harmed me. Even when he had the opportunity to escape, he stayed and protected me. He feels an attachment to me. Let me go in there and help him so we can show Lord va'Rin that we're honoring his wishes, even when we have to go above and beyond the normal call of duty."

"She's crazy," one of the guards in the back mutters.

But I've got Kennak's attention now. He gazes thoughtfully at Victor's cell, and I know he's turning it over in his head. He doesn't like the situation, but he's ambitious, and he won't want to disappoint Lord va'Rin.

"You've got great big weapons," I say enthusiastically. "If I look like I'm in the slightest bit of danger, you can use them, right? You can activate his collar—a collar he's wearing voluntarily, I might add—and shut him down. I'm not in real danger." I put a hand on his sleeve. "But he is in *real* distress. And I want to help him."

Kennak stares at Victor's form in the cell. His back is still to us, but his shoulders are hunched tight, his hands digging at the tile at his feet. He thinks for a long, long moment, until I worry he's going to tell me no. Instead, he looks down at me and sighs heavily. "You realize this is foolhardy."

"He won't hurt me," I point out again. "We both know that."

"When he's in his right mind, he won't, no. But he's not in his right mind right now, Bee."

"Which is why you fine gentlemen are here to protect me," I say sweetly. "Just...please. Let me do this. I promised him I was on his side. I want to show him that I truly am."

He sighs again. "I'm a keffing idiot." But he moves away from the door panel. "If there's even a hint of danger—"

"I know," I say quickly. "I understand. Victor won't hurt me though." I don't tell them it's because he wants to kiss me. Because we have an agreement. Right now I'm not sure if he even remembers our agreement. Maybe he's not in his right mind, like Kennak said. But he's in distress, and I have to try. I can't leave him like this.

I move toward the door, watching the guards. They hold their weapons tightly but no one stops me, so I remind myself that I must truly be safe if they're going to let me do this. If Riffin was here, he would pitch a fit, but...would he? I wonder, because I've been so used to managing everyone to get my way that I don't know if that's the case. Maybe he'd let me waltz into Victor's cell anyhow and not say a thing. I put my hand on the door panel and lift my head so the security computers can do a retinal scan. I wait for anxiety or nervousness to kick in, but the only thing I feel right now is worry for Victor. What's happening with him? How can I help?

The door opens, and I hear the sound of a half-dozen stun-rifles sing to life. Right. I have to play this carefully. If I panic, I don't want anyone shooting Victor by mistake. "It's Bee," I say softly. "I'm coming in to talk to you, Victor. Please don't make any sudden moves, all right?"

"Bee," he grits out again, and it sounds as if my name is coming through clenched teeth. Mercy. His tail shivers, and I can't tell if it's with fury or something else. But he doesn't move, which is a good sign. He just remains where he is, hunched in the middle of the floor.

I take a step forward and the door slides shut behind me. It takes everything I have not to jump, and I clench my hands at my sides. Then I realize that's not exactly the pose of a relaxed person, so I force my sweaty fists to release and smooth my hands on the skirt of my tunic. "I'm taking a few steps across the room," I say, dictating aloud my movements. "I don't have any weapons with me, or any food. It's just me and my bare hands, all right? But once we figure out what's bothering you, we'll get you the regular treats I bring."

He doesn't move. If anything, his shoulders get stiffer, and his fingers clench against the floor. The maddening screech of claws against marble ends.

I take that as an encouraging sign. I take a few more slow, deliberate steps forward, talking the entire time. "It's just waffles today, but you like those, right? I got home late last night so there wasn't a lot of time to do anything elaborate. If you like, though, I can make you something better tonight to bring in tomorrow. You just have to tell me what you prefer." I keep my voice soft and even, speaking slowly as I take even slower steps forward. "Did you eat breakfast or were you waiting for me to arrive?"

I'm practically at his side at this point, and he hasn't moved. Encouraging. Whatever is bothering him, he doesn't want to hurt me. That's a good sign. A great sign, actually. I'm so relieved that it makes me want to rush forward, but I continue taking mincing, small steps as I shuffle my way toward him, my actions deliberate. A sudden movement might be his death or mine, and I'm acutely aware of that.

I go to stand in front of Victor, and study him with confusion. His gaze is downcast, his big body trembling slightly. His mouth is covered in froth, strings of drool hanging from his mouth. His muscles are hunched, as if he's...bracing himself? Is he fighting something in his head? I don't get it—all I know is that something is wrong. "Victor," I breathe. "I'm here."

He looks up at me, and our eyes meet.

Victor's eyes are completely flooded with red.

11

BEE

I gasp at the sight of his eyes.

They're blood red, the sclera a dark and angry scarlet. Back when I first started this job, I'd been told that Victor's eyes—Crulden's eyes—would flood with red when he went berserk. I'd almost forgotten about that tidbit, because he's been more or less calm around me. Moody, yes, but never violent. He looks terrifying like this, his eyes full of danger and madness. I fight back the surge of terror I feel because he doesn't look like Victor in this moment. He looks like the monster they want him to be.

And I know that's simply not true. He wants to be better. He doesn't want to attack...because we have a deal. He's going to play along with all of this...and I'm going to kiss him. I know Victor well enough at this point to know that he wants that kiss. He hasn't said as much, but it's been obvious in the way he watches me, in the way he obsesses over my scent, over when Riffin touches me.

He wanted that kiss more than escaping.

Which is why this sudden madness doesn't make sense. What—or who—is pushing him toward berserking? Towards losing the control he's been so careful to keep for this last while, all for the promise of a kiss from someone like me? "Victor," I say softly as those blood-filled eyes lock onto me. "Am I in danger right now, being in here with you?"

He pants, hard. But that's all he does. His fingers dig into the floor again, desperately clawing at the tile.

"I'm going to take that as a no." I pitch my voice low, as if we're sharing secrets. "But you need to talk to me if you can, Victor. Let me help you."

Victor's nostrils flare and his tail lashes. His entire posture is one of danger and I worry that the guards are going to get trigger happy and make matters worse.

So I decide to be a little daring. "Let me help you," I say again, and lift my hands slowly towards his face. His eyes are wild and his mouth slack. A string of drool hangs from one terrifying-looking tusk, but he doesn't look fearsome to me. My heart is squeezing with sympathy instead, because I want to help him. He's obviously distressed. "I'm not leaving you. I'm going to stay at your side and we're going to figure this out, because we're friends." I lift my hands toward his cheeks and move to cup them. "And because we have a deal—"

The moment my skin comes in contact with his, a rush of painful, snapping electricity crashes through me. I cry out as a torrent of pain flares from his body into mine. It feels as if a brick wall slams into me as I go crashing backward.

"Get her out of there," someone shouts. "Light him up!"

Oh no. No, no that's not what I wanted at all. Dizzy, I try to sit up. Everything in my body feels as if it's been pounded to dust. There's a smell of something singed, which I suspect is me. My ears are ringing and the shouts of the guards sound very far away. Rough hands grab my arms, hauling me upright.

My head feels like it's full of slush as I get to my feet, but my legs don't feel strong enough to hold me. What—

"Don't touch her!"

The snarl comes from Victor. A moment later, the guard holding me upright goes flying as Victor grabs him by the collar and flings him aside. A moment later, he braces his hands over me, against the wall. We've been in this pose before, and as I look up at Victor's terrifying face, his red eyes are focused on me and only me.

"Bee," he manages. "Can't...touch me. Not...safe."

"Someone get that shock collar activated," the captain yells. "My control isn't working!"

"Captain, sir, we are," cries one of the guards. "All of ours are turned on. It's not working!"

Victor stares down at me, his blood-filled eyes wide and distant. He trembles overhead, his nails digging into the walls of his cell. It's like he's desperately trying to keep control. A split second later, I realize that's exactly what he's doing. The shock-guns aren't activating because his collar is already at full blast.

He's being tortured.

"I'm here," I tell him softly. "I won't leave you." In a louder voice, I call out, "Someone get First Rank Novis! His collar is malfunctioning!"

12

VICTOR

*W*hen the pain falls away, it feels like a trick. To go from a full night of endless pain, unable to function without agony to...silence? To relief? It takes time for it to sink in, and when it does, I collapse to my knees. I don't want to —I don't want to show weakness in front of anyone—but there's no strength left in me. It took everything I had not to claw off my own face, not to fling myself at the walls and break through to kill the hated guards that were doing this to me.

The only thing that kept me from losing my grasp on sanity was the realization that Bee would not stand for this. Bee would be mad when she found out. Bee, who is going to kiss me as long as I uphold my end of our bargain.

So I hold out for Bee.

I'm grateful I did. The moment she can touch me without sharing the shocking pain, she does. Her soft hands flutter over my face and shoulders, and then she's barking orders at the guardsmen as if she's the one in charge. They get a damp towel.

They get fresh water for me, and warm broth to sip. They get a fluffy blanket and wrap it around me, and then Bee cradles my head in her lap, caressing my cheek with the backs of her fingers.

It's the best thing I've ever felt. I never want to leave this moment. I close my eyes and pretend to be unconscious, unthreatening, all so they'll let Bee stay with me as long as possible.

It's hard to remain "unconscious" when she starts scolding people, though.

"How could you let this happen?" Bee demands when First Rank Novis enters my cell. I can tell it's him by the scent of his uniform and the whiff of tea that remains on his breath. "How did no one bother to check to see if his collar was hurting him? I thought you were interested in his well-being!"

"Now, female." His voice takes on a patient tone. "You—"

"Don't you 'now female' me," Bee says indignantly. Her tiny hand cups my jaw, as if she can protect me from him. I want to remind her that she's forgetting to be pleasant, but I'm too fascinated by her anger. "Lord va'Rin wants this man reformed, yes? I'm not seeing a lot of reforming, First Rank. I'm seeing bullying and torture. If you don't want me to run screaming to the lord about how he's being mistreated, you'll get me some answers. And frankly? You want me on your side. I can make life *very* difficult for you."

I've never heard such an angry tone come out of such a soft female.

"I can assure you, this wasn't done on purpose—"

"How did his collar malfunction?" Bee asks. "How did no one think to check on it?"

"Female—"

"It wasn't a malfunction, was it? That's what you're pussy-footing around. Someone turned his collar up to maximum because they wanted to hurt him." Her fingers stroke my jaw and I bite back the groan of pleasure that nearly escapes me. Her touch is maddening in just how good it feels. "Someone tortured him on purpose."

There's a long pause as she continues to pet me. "We don't know for certain—"

Her voice is bitter. "You do. You just don't want to admit it." Bee's fingers pause. "Is...was it Riffin? The timing's a little too coincidental."

"We'd have to review security logs to be certain," First Rank Novis says in that bland, condescending voice of his. Underneath that, though, he's starting to smell stale. It's a fear smell, like he knows he's messed up and isn't quite sure how to fix the situation.

It's almost worth the last night of agony just to know he's sweating over my well-being.

Bee's fingers dance along my cheekbone, then move along the ridge of my nose as if she's memorizing my features with her fingertips. It's a delicate touch, one that I find as confusing as I do addicting. My mind is full of swarms of memories, most of which, I'm realizing, are not mine. The old master I thought I had? That was the other Crulden, as are the fragments of screaming females, of war prizes that I treated badly. I try not to think about those moments, because I imagined Bee in them once, and it nearly made me sick.

I've been cloned from a monster. Bee should stay away from me...but I don't want her to. I want her to keep touching me, because I'm selfish and greedy.

"I think it was Riffin," Bee says softly as she runs her fingers over my thick brows. "I think it was Riffin and he's getting back at me by hurting Victor."

"As I said, I'll look into the security logs—"

Bee talks right over him again, her gentle voice full of authority. "I also think Victor will never have a chance to get better in this particular situation. He's not in a cage anymore, but your people are still treating him like an animal. He needs a different environment, and I'm going to tell Lord va'Rin that."

The stale sweat scent coats First Rank Novis, and I suspect he's imagining his job going up in flames. "Then what do you propose, female?"

I wait for Bee to chide him again for calling her that—she hates that "female" word—but she doesn't. Instead, her tone turns sweet. Managing. "I want Victor set up with a house of his own. He can be given over to my care. I'll be his companion until he's learned everything he can."

Her finger strokes the corner of my mouth, and my cock twitches to alertness.

"Absolutely not—"

"You can set sentries," Bee continues on as if Novis has no authority in this. "But they have to stay at least a hundred feet away from Victor's house at all times. He needs room to breathe. He needs to not feel like a prisoner. Because if this continues, you're going to lose him, and he's trying so very hard to be a good man."

My cock hardens even more at the affection in her voice. She thinks I am...good? Why does that please me so very much?

"You think this will work?" Novis asks.

"I think it's worth a try," Bee says. "And when Lord va'Rin asks for a status report on Victor, we'll have positive things to tell him instead of discussing how the guards are torturing him." She traces my lip briefly, then goes back to my jaw. "He needs to go somewhere he won't be bothered. So he can relax and be himself without fear of reprisal."

"And I'm supposed to send a vulnerable human female to stay with him? Everyone will think I've given you to him to ensure his good behavior. They'll think you're..." His voice drops. "...romantic."

I wait for Bee to protest or make a sound of disgust. "Victor and I are friends," she finally says. "I don't care what they think." She stretches, her lap shifting, and I suspect she's turned to look at Novis. "Do we have an agreement?"

"Do I have a choice?" He knows the human has the upper hand, and he hates it.

"One last thing," Bee says in that managing tone of hers. "Make sure you don't tell Riffin. I think Victor needs all new guards. The same ones, over and over again, so he can learn to trust them. He needs a fresh start."

First Rank Novis just sighs heavily, and I know Bee has won.

13

VICTOR

I keep expecting the cuffs and a collar—or even a cage —to come out as we're readied to leave. Plans are made as Bee speaks with Novis, and a trunk full of supplies is ordered into the nearest air-sled. Two volunteer guards are going to be sent with us, and though their scents are tinged with a hint of uncertainty, there's not overwhelming fear.

It's probably due to Bee's presence. Bee, who stands proudly at my side, holding my enormous hand in her small one. She gazes at them all fiercely, my determined protector. She hasn't left my side once. She insists on others coming in to take care of us, bringing food and water, and clutches my hand the entire time as if to reassure me of her presence.

Then Novis is finally ready, and we're escorted out of the building that's been my "home" for the last two months and into the open.

The moment we step outside, I pause, stunned at the scent of the open air. It's raining, and the constant pounding of small droplets on the building's metallic roof was something that my memories told me I knew. But coming outside and breathing in the damp air, rich with the scent of wet dirt and grass, was an entirely different experience. I stop in my tracks, tilting my face up to the sky, and the cool rain pounds on my skin, soaking me.

It feels...amazing. Even my borrowed memories don't have anything like this. I close my eyes and just enjoy.

"Guards," Novis says warily.

"It's okay," Bee tells him. "Give him a moment."

I don't open my eyes or move. Even if they stab me with a dozen shock-sticks, I want to appreciate this sensation for as long as I can. It's rare that I have pleasures in my life. My mind is filled with all bad things and...I want more of *this* sort of thing.

"Why is he stopping, female?"

"He's enjoying the rain," Bee says reasonably. "Give him a moment." She squeezes my hand again, letting me know that everything is fine. "He has a name, First Rank. You can always ask him."

The male makes a disgruntled sound. Finally, he speaks. "Move it along, Crulden. You can enjoy the rain at your new home."

Bee sneezes.

It's that tiny sneeze that gets me moving. I keep forgetting that humans are fragile, and for all that Bee can be formidable when she's crossed, she still needs protecting. This rain is probably cold and unpleasant to her. So I open my eyes, shake the droplets off my mane, and nod at the guardsmen. As we get in the air-sled, the constant patter of rain on the windows is familiar, and I watch the countryside move quickly underneath us as we travel. Bee and I are in the back seat of the sled, with the two guardsmen flying the machine. I'm not sad to leave First Rank Novis behind.

Bee sneezes again and then sniffles. When I look over at

her, she gives me a watery smile, the tip of her nose flushed a deeper shade than the rest of her skin. "Allergies. There's something in the soil here that bothers me. It's more noticeable when it rains, but I'll be fine."

She told me about her allergies before, once, when she was making idle talk, explaining to me why she wanted to be a "social worker" for the humans instead of farming. "This is why you do not have land."

"Right. I'd have to farm, and since I can't, I do what I can." She shrugs, her hand damp in mine. "I don't really mind most times, though it'd be nice to have a place to call my own. I can't be selfish about it, though, especially not with new humans coming in all the time."

I think about this, about how unselfish she is, how giving. She gets no reward for helping me—other than to take a job that will allow her to help other humans. Her spirit is good and pure, and she deserves better than to be touched by a monster like me. But since I am a monster, I am going to take as much of her as I can. Now that my fascination with rain is waning slightly, I can focus on thoughts of Bee.

We're going to be alone together for the first time.

I'm going to claim that kiss she promised.

14

BEE

*A*fter all the rolling plains and endless, flat-looking farms, I'm surprised to see that we're driven up to a small, double-domed house on the edge of a tall cliff. The guards park the sled in front and then grab the trunk of supplies from the back and proceed to carry it away from the house. At my confused look, one explains, "This is where we're staying. You're farther down."

"Oh. Of course." I smile brightly at them. "Lead the way."

It's still raining, and my clothes are soaked. I'm doing my best not to sneeze again, but I can feel my sinuses filling up, my nose itching and my eyes watering. Victor has been quiet for a while now, and I hope this isn't too overwhelming for him. For a brief, wild moment I wonder if I'm doing the right thing. Am I putting my life in danger? No one else in the universe trusts Victor, who's been cloned from one of the nastiest monsters to ever grace an arena. I've heard enough about Crulden the Ruiner in the last few weeks to last a lifetime.

I glance over at my companion. One hand is still in mine, but the other is upturned to the sky, catching rain. He stares at the water on his hand with fascination, and my heart squeezes at that small joy. Everyone else in the universe is wrong about him, I decide. He just wants to be free to live his life, like anyone else that's been fucked over by the greedy machinations of the galaxy. I'm going to give him that chance.

The guards carry the crate along a winding path close to the edge of the cliffs. If I look down over the edge, I see a fast-flowing river, full of rocks and dangerous, white-foamed rapids. It looks awfully high, but surely they wouldn't send us out here just to drown, so I have to assume it's fine.

At a rocky outcropping, there's a squat, square sort of building right on the edge of the cliff. It's ugly and boxy and metal and looks a bit like a storage building from back home, but something tells me that this is our new temporary home. There's a pair of large windows at the front, framing an equally square door, and an old, abandoned planter box hangs off one of the windows.

"Is this someone's home?" I ask politely. "I'd hate to displace anyone." I also didn't think to ask if Victor and I would be alone. I'd just assumed we would after Novis mentioned the guards would be staying a short distance away. I don't know how Victor's going to react if we're staying with another woman.

The guards set the trunk down on the step, panting, and one shakes his head, rain flicking off his metallic horns. I don't know his name. "This place is abandoned. When Lord va'Rin had houses built for the humans, he called in some contractors to build dwellings evenly spaced apart. They built this one, but a human can't live here alone, so the female was relocated somewhere else."

I glance around at the land. The house is smack-dab on the edge of the cliff, which is worrying, but spread out nearby, I also don't see a lot of farmland. I see rocky grounds without a lot of greenery, but not much soil to till. "She couldn't live here because of the inability to farm?"

"Nah," says the other guard, Herrix. "It's the pump house. Too weak to crank it."

"Pump house?" I inquire. I'm starting to get cold, the rain making my clothing feel ten times heavier than it is. It clings to my skin and I just want to go inside and change, but I also don't want to pressure Victor into taking this house if it isn't right for our needs.

His needs, I remind myself. I'm just here to help out. It's not an "us" thing.

"Yup. Pump house. This house has flood potential, so when the river gets too high, someone has to crank the pump house manually. It diverts the water to an underground reservoir that filters the water and then sends it to Port. That's why you're here." Herrix puts his hands on his hips, clearly beat down by the ceaseless rain. "First Rank figures you're a good walking distance away from the closest farm, and as long as you stay on top of the river, you're fine. It's nice and quiet."

I nod slowly, then look up at Victor. I'm still holding his hand, which makes me feel a little shy, but no one's said anything about it. "Do you think you can handle the pump house?"

His thick, furry brows go up and then he leans in close to me. "I'm confident I'm stronger than a human female, if that's what you are asking."

I snort with amusement. "I just wanted to make sure it was a task you wanted to take on."

Victor straightens, the look on his dangerous face turning determined. "I will be the best at handling the pump house, wait and see."

Right. Because he's a champion and he does nothing by halves.

HERRIX AND AKRIS, the two guards assigned to us, show us both how to work the pump house. It's a small building at the back of the large, square one, built on a platform hanging over the lip of the cliff. Below the platform, I can see a massive network of tubes, each one big enough to swallow Victor whole, that disappear into the rock. The pump house itself is a series of manually cranking wheels, which seems strange to me in this technologically advanced world, but perhaps it's something that doesn't need to run all the time and therefore is more cost-efficient this way. Don't know, don't care. Victor cranks the first wheel with ease and then cranks the next one, and the look of smug pleasure on his face makes me bite back a laugh.

But then the guards say their goodbyes and let me know that they're just down the path at the round-domed house, and that the comm inside the square house is programmed with their contact information, so all I need to do is hit a button if I require help. They take the air-sled with them and go, and then I'm left, standing in the rain, with Victor.

Alone.

He's watching me closely, his mane streaming water, his skin soaked. The trou he's wearing are shredded (as was the back seat of the air-sled, thanks to his spikes) and he looks intimidatingly large and muscular wet like this. I wipe the dampness from my face and smile brightly at him. "Shall we check out our accommodations, then?"

"Are you scared to be alone with me?"

"Not at all." I'm not, either. I feel...something? But it's not fear. It might be a hint of anticipation. This could be the break-through that Victor needs. That's what I tell myself, at least. I'm not going to prod at the other reasons I might be feeling anticipation, not with him at my side and able to sniff out everything. When he looks a little skeptical, I raise my hand in the air and pull back my sleeve. "If you don't believe me, smell me."

Victor takes a step forward and clasps my wrist, his nose less than an inch away from my skin as he delicately sniffs me. That shouldn't make me feel things. It's just that he looks like he wants to lick the inside of my wrist, and that thought makes hot little tendrils flare deep inside me.

He leans in closer, and my breath hitches as he ever-so-lightly runs his nose against my wet skin. "We should go inside," I breathe, unable to take my eyes off him. "It's raining."

Victor's focus is entirely on my skin, and I can't tear my gaze away from him. He's so very fascinated by that part of me. I wonder if it smells better than the rest of my body. Or is it the trace of veins he sees under the delicate skin there? Or—

His expression changes as he gazes at my arm. His tail thrashes while the rest of him goes still, and then I realize what he's looking at. One of my finger-shaped bruises is peeping out of my wet sleeve.

Oh no.

Victor's eyes start to turn red again, even as he fixes his gaze on me. "Who—"

"No one here," I say quickly. "It was an accident, and it's taken care of."

His nostrils flare and he sniffs the air. I'm not sure how much he can scent in a downpour, but my heart plummets when he pulls my sleeve further back, revealing the wealth of bruises Riffin left up and down my arm. Victor takes one deep, shuddering breath. Then another.

"If you lose control, you're proving them right," I whisper. "Just remember that."

The look he gives me is pure frustration, mingled with fury. I expect him to lose it. To just freak out and attack everything and anything in sight. To chase down the guards that just left us and fling them over the cliffs. Whatever he can do to cause chaos and misery on my behalf, even if I don't want it.

Instead, he closes his eyes and pauses for a moment. He runs his thumb lightly over the inside of my wrist, his claw avoiding my skin, and then he releases me.

I sneeze.

I can practically see his hackles go up, his triangular-shaped ears perking. He fixes his gaze on me again. "You are going to go inside and get warm," he tells me. "And then we are going to talk."

Sounds somewhat reasonable. I nod and head for the door, rubbing my twitching nose. Maybe I can feign catching a cold to distract him from the bruises. Act weak and whiny and help-less to pull his interest towards something else, or at least stall. It's just that it feels rather disingenuous and unfair to manipu-late Victor like I do everyone else. It feels like we're on the same team most of the time, and I'm loath to lose that feeling.

Better to just come clean and get it over with.

I glance over at Victor and as I watch, he grabs the enor-mous trunk that took two full-sized mesakkah to carry and slings it over one shoulder as if it weighs nothing. He grunts at me, gesturing at the door with his other hand.

Right. Inside. I shouldn't stare at that display of strength or the way his muscles are defined by the pouring rain. I blink my eyes to clear them and open the door, stepping over the threshold.

I gasp the moment I step inside, because it's not what I expected at all. The exterior of the house is plain and sterile, but it's obvious that whatever human lived here for a short period of time did their best to make this place a cozy home. The usual generic accoutrements are here—a small fridge, a food processor, a comm panel on one wall, a sad-looking chair and table in the living area. But the walls...oh, the walls.

The walls have been painted in bright, enticing patterns.

One wall is nothing but circular flowers in reds and yellows and oranges, sunny splashes of color intermixed with paler paisley shapes. The small adjacent kitchen is painted with blue stars and yellow moons tumbling all over the exposed wall space, and I race toward the bedroom with excitement, because I can't wait to see what beauty is there.

The walls there are decorated too, but it's full of hearts and butterflies, and I blush at all the pink adorning the walls. Maybe I should have seen that coming. At any rate, it's delightful. Is it a little childish? Sure. A little overly bright? Yes. But it's so happy and warm that I adore it, and it changes my impression of the somber building entirely. "How delightful," I say as I hear Victor come in behind me. "The person that painted all this must have been so devastated to leave it all behind."

"Or," he says slowly, setting the trunk down, "They were pleased to have entirely new walls to paint."

I blink in surprise, because that's the most positive thing I've ever heard come from him. "Why Victor, you ray of sunshine."

He shoves the trunk against one of the walls and then steps toward me. "You're wet."

That makes me blink again, because something completely different comes to mind, and it takes me a moment to realize he's referring to my clothes and water. I clear my throat, suddenly very aware of the small house and Victor's huge presence. "We did stand outside in the rain for a while."

Victor stalks past me, opening one of the doors, scanning the inside of an empty closet, and then shutting it again. "Blankets. Where?"

Oh. Right. "Let's open the trunk. It looks like one of the settlement packages they give to human women when they're assigned a farm." I smile brightly at him and move toward the enormous box, touching the panel to open it. Sure enough, inside are dried pantry goods and household basics. I pick up the plas-wrapped blanket and hold the bundle out to him, then dig around for another. Hmm. Just one. Come to think of it, there had only been one small bed, too.

This...was not thought through very well. I frown, digging in the trunk a little deeper in case I missed anything. Soaps. Cleaning supplies. Menstrual supplies. A metal pot and a couple of mugs. "There's only one blanket." I get to my feet, plucking at the wet clothing that's sticking to my body and outlining my every roll and dimple. "I'll go speak to Herrix and tell him we need more—"

Victor steps between me and the door. He pushes the blanket toward me. "You take it. I'm not cold."

I'm not cold either, just uncomfortable, but my nose chooses that moment to tickle, and I sneeze again. Victor's features take on a stubborn look and he moves toward me, tugging at my collar.

I make a sound of alarm as he does, slapping his big hands away. "What are you doing?"

"Helping you undress." He says it gruffly, the annoyance still threading through his voice. "Then you are going to wrap up in the blanket and you're going to tell me about those bruises."

"Maybe I don't want to talk about the bruises," I say, pushing his hands away when he reaches for my collar again. "They really are none of your business."

"You don't want to talk about the bruises?" Victor's voice turns into a growl, and he scowls down at me. His eyes aren't red, though, so I take that as a good sign. "Fine. Then I want my champion's reward."

My brain must not be firing on all cylinders, because I have no idea what he's talking about. "Your champion's reward?" I echo. "What reward?"

He leans in, all tusks and teeth and bright, bright eyes. "My kiss. You said you'd kiss me if I went along with things." He gestures at our surroundings. "Here I am, not drinking the blood of my enemies. I am being docile...and I want my kiss. I want us to share breath."

I flush, a flutter of excitement in my belly at his demand. "Right now?"

"No," he says, and puts his hand on the bundled blanket, plucking it out of my grip and holding it in front of my face. "You are going to get under this without your clothes on. And then we are going to kiss. I have been very patient."

I swallow hard, my pulse thundering. "You're being very demanding," I say, but I take the blanket from him again and unwrap the plas-film covering off of it. The blanket underneath isn't very soft, but it's functional. "What if I were to tell you that I don't appreciate your tone and that I want you to speak to me like a friend? And that you don't make demands of friends?"

Victor leans in, bending over an absurd amount to try and come eye to eye with me. "I would agree with you. But I would also point out that you're stubborn and used to pushing others into giving you what you want, and that ends with me. We're equals."

"Fair enough." I point at the bathroom. "But I'm changing in there."

15

VICTOR

*B*ee smells keffing amazing.

I draw in great lungfuls of air, loving the slight scent that threads through the stale scent of the house. Even that's not so bad. There's a faint whiff of someone here long ago, the smell of dust, and everything else is Bee. Bee, whose scent has been growing steadily more enticing by the moment. Bee, who smells like faint arousal and curiosity, and the arousal part is growing more intense by the moment.

She did not like the rain quite like I did. Even now, I'm tempted to go out and stand in it once more, just to feel it on my face. It felt fresh, and new, and different. I love it, even though I've done my best to hide how much I liked it. Bee seemed less thrilled, and it made her sneeze, so I want her indoors. I'm tempted to race outside and see how far I can get before they catch me—always, always in the back of my head, there is a need to escape, to break free, to test the boundaries of my captivity. But I made a promise to Bee, and she is going to kiss me and let her breath mingle with mine, so I put off the escape once more.

I look around the small house for somewhere to sit. Nothing here is sized appropriately for me. It has been made for humans, and even the uncomfortable-looking metal chair in the living area looks barely big enough to hold Bee and will certainly not hold my weight. I glance in the bedroom, and the bed is narrow and short. My feet would hang off the end, provided that I did not destroy the mattress the moment I laid down.

There is only one bed.

It belongs to Bee, then. If she is staying with me, I want her comfortable. It is only right. She has given up all her freedom to be my companion, so the least I can do is give her the bed. I stare at it, and stare, my thoughts sliding toward that bed over and over again. She would not let me share it with her...would she?

It is ridiculous to even entertain such a thought, and I quickly push it out of my mind. I am a champion, I remind myself. I succeed at competitions and strive to win rewards. I have not thought further than this kiss, but...what if Bee does not like it? What if she is revolted by my mouth on hers?

If so, I do not think I would want more kisses. My mind floods with Crulden's fragmented memories, of females screaming and doing their best to race away as I chase after them, thrilled by their cries, their terror—

I shake my head and pace, trying to clear my thoughts. I must think of other things.

I will talk to Bee in the morning. Perhaps she will help me determine new rewards, after we share breath. If I disgust her, we will need to think of a new set of goals for me, a new series of prizes to be won. It is important to me that I make her proud. That she likes me. Bee's opinion is the only one that matters to me in all the galaxy.

"Hey Victor?" Bee calls from the lavatory. "I don't have a change of clothes with me, so I'm coming out in the blanket. You promise me that I can trust you?"

I am puzzled. What is not to trust in this moment? I look around, but I do not see anything that looks like a weapon. "I do not see what the two have to do with one another. Trust me with what?"

"You know."

"I assure you, Bee, I do not know."

"Can I trust you not to try and take the blanket from me?" Her voice is against the door, as if she is pressing against it.

Why would I take it from her? "I do not wish the blanket. I am not cold."

The door to the lavatory opens a crack, and Bee peeks out. "I mean...don't steal the blanket to try and look at my body, all right?"

I give her an incredulous look. Does she truly think I would do such a thing just to gaze at her teats and cunt? I am more interested in her mind and her thoughts...and that invitingly soft mouth of hers. "If I wished to see your body, Bee, I would not have insisted you get out of your clothes. I would have suggested you stay in them. They were wet enough that they showed everything."

"Great, thanks for that," she mutters. I hear fabric rustle, and then she gives a little sigh before opening the door fully. Bee gives me a dubious look, her wet hair hanging in damp waves around her rounded face. "I don't suppose hiding behind this door actually does anything anyhow."

"It is true. I could break it down easily."

Bee makes a frustrated little sound. "Of course you could." She sweeps out of the bathroom, clutching the blanket around her like a cloak. It hides her body from my view except for a glimpse of her neck and a bit of enticing-looking skin at her collarbones. Better than anything is her scent. I nearly stagger as it washes over me.

There's a definite thread of arousal wafting through her normally pleasant smell and it's making me crazy. My skin itches and the urge to pace, to flick my tail, to do something, moves all over me. It's a restless energy I don't know how to utilize. I fist my hands and then unclench them, not wanting to seem intimidating to her.

"What's wrong?" she asks, worried. "You seem agitated."

I *am* agitated. I do not know why. Or rather, I know she is affecting me and I do not know how to handle it. "Something about me is...unsettled right now. Urgent." I clench my fists again. "I feel like I need to..." I trail off, because I do not know what I need, other than to grasp my cock and pound it to release some of what I am feeling.

Either that or tear a few throats out.

"Is it me?" Bee asks, hitching the blanket tighter around her damp skin. "Should I go?"

I shake my head violently. "If you do...I will chase you."

I expect her to get upset—or afraid—at my words. But Bee only wrinkles her nose. "It's not much of a chase. You could catch me in three breaths."

That is the point. Of course then what would I do with her once I have her? Watch her recoil in disgust from my touch? I know I do not look like the mesakkah, with their decorated horns and strong faces. I am different and hideous. I have big teeth. I am covered in spikes. I drool, because my mouth does not properly close over my tusks. Bee would hate being touched by me.

That is why I am agitated.

I want her and I know I cannot have her. Bee is soft and pretty and smells so keffing good she makes my mouth water. She is clever and wily and any male would want to claim her as a mate. She could have her pick of the males here—and she has

Riffin, who makes her cunt remain dry as bone. She drifts with arousal near me...but is it for me? Or one of the other guards?

I war with my thoughts.

If I make her share breath with me, then I will know for sure if this arousal scent is for me. But if I kiss her and she is disgusted, I will lose her forever. I will not have anything to reach for any longer, and without an incentive, I will not feel that urgent need to win. I will kef things up and then Bee will abandon me.

I want Bee's friendship more than I want her kiss, I realize. I want both, but if I have to choose, I will choose Bee's affection. I crave the sound of her voice and her gentle laughter more than anything else in the universe. I know that when Bee is near and smiling, that everything is all right. I need that in my life more than I need a few unwilling kisses.

It pains me to admit, "We need a new bargain."

Bee isn't paying attention to my words. She's watching me pace, her small, dark brows furrowed. "Won't you sit down, Victor?"

I shake my head, distracted. "There is no good place for me to sit. This house is made for humans. But you and I, we should—"

"Nonsense," Bee says, and that bossy tone is in her voice. She gestures at the chair. "This won't work for you?"

I eye it, amused that I am yet again at her command, despite my vows to do otherwise. "Do you truly think it will hold me?"

She studies the chair. "No, I guess you're right. Well, that's frustrating. The bed is probably the wrong size, too." She moves past me in the small house, studying the furniture, and then her gaze alights on the spilled-open trunk. She bends over next to it, rummaging through the contents, and I catch a glimpse of brown bosom and deep cleavage and I have been lying to myself, because I do want to see what is under that blanket... but only if she wants to show me.

Bee grabs a fist-sized plas-wrapped package with an "aha" and holds it out to me, her free hand still clutching her blanket closed. "Do me a favor and open that."

I do as she asks and the compressed item spills into my hands, fluffing up. It's a pillow, like the one that she insisted they give me for my bedding, even though I have no memories of using one in the past.

Bee shuts the trunk, turns around and promptly takes the pillow out of my hands and then sets it atop the trunk with a pat. "There. Now you have a decent seat until we can get something else figured out."

Sit on her pillow? But it is for her head. "Bee, I cannot do that."

"Why? Do you have spikes on your butt? I didn't think you did." Her pulse thrums, speeding up, and I wonder what about my spikes makes her heart race. Fear? She tries to peek around me, to look at my backside.

"It is your pillow." I pick it up and offer it to her. "You need it."

Bee takes it from my hands and puts it back on the trunk. "You need someplace comfortable to sit more than I need a pillow. I'll be fine without one. Now sit down before I start screaming at you."

I laugh at the image of the delicate human shrieking in my face in frustration. "No, you won't."

But she's gone still. She gazes up at me, wide-eyed. "Did you just laugh, Victor?"

I scowl, because she's making me nervous.

Bee's look is one of delight, though. She beams up at me and plants her hand on my chest. "Don't be so grouchy. I like your laughter. It sounds happy, and it's the first time I've heard it. Of course it's going to make me pause. Now sit, and you can tell me what's troubling you."

"I am not troubled," I say, even as I sit down atop the trunk.

With the pillow, it is rather comfortable. "I just do not like taking things that should be for you."

"And you're not." She reaches out and brushes a wet strand of my mane back from my eyes and then draws back. "Sorry. I'm not trying to get in your face. It just looked like it was bothering you." She bites her lip. "You're soaked and here I am holding the only blanket."

I shrug. "As I said, it does not bother me."

"But something's troubling you. You said you wanted a new...reward?" Our eyes meet and I realize that when I am seated like this, we are practically the same height, she and I. Strange to think that she is so small, and yet she is utterly unafraid of me. She is my friend, a friend that watches me with gentle, worried eyes. "Talk to me, Victor. Let me help you."

Hesitating, I finally answer. "I have asked for something you do not want to give, and my memories are full of other times." I pause. "Times when...when I took what was not freely given."

Bee's look is one of confusion, then realization. Her hand goes to my arm and she touches me, ever so gentle. Her hand feels so good on my skin that I think I would endure a thousand more electric shocks just for that touch. "That wasn't you," she says. "Those memories are in your head, but that was a different person. You're just a clone of his. You're not him."

"I know."

"But these memories...they distress you anyhow?"

I nod.

"And that's why you don't want to kiss me," she states, seeking confirmation.

"You said once before you did not wish to kiss me. I do not want to force you into doing something you do not want to do... even though I know I would be good at it."

Bee blinks at me and then giggles. One eyebrow goes up. "You'd be good at it, huh?"

"I'd be the best," I say confidently. "I am a champion. But if you do not want to kiss, I will need a new prize, because I value you, Bee. I do not want to harm you." And it would bother me if her cunt remained dry when I kissed her, like it did with her other male. I know I would be excellent at it, but if there is no desire on her end, it does not matter how good I am.

I have smelled her cunt, but maybe she likes my words and not my face. Maybe words are as far as she wants to go.

She studies my face, scrutinizing my features. Her gaze falls to my mouth and I hate that it is stretched wide over my tusks, that it is not firm and closed. Maybe that is why she hesitates. Maybe she finds me revolting. I consider all the things she might dislike about me, and I almost miss her response. "Perhaps...perhaps I want to try kissing you."

It's not what I expected. "You do?"

Her arousal scent floods the air around me, and her breathing speeds up. The hunter in me notices these things, and I am utterly fascinated. I want her to step nearer. I want her to move close enough that I can bury my face against her throat and just breathe in her delicious smell.

"I just don't know if I'll like it," Bee continues, a troubled expression on her face. "You have to understand my past."

"Then tell me. I wish to know."

Her scent changes, souring with nervousness. She glances around the room. "This might take a minute. I should probably sit down." Bee's gaze fixes on the chair across the room, the one I did not even bother to try. She considers it for a moment and then looks back at me. "Can I sit on your lap?"

She does not even have to ask. Hot pleasure thrums through me, and I manage a nod. Bee puts a hand on my knee, and my entire body reacts to that small touch. She only pushes my thighs apart and then steps between them, settling her soft bottom on top of one of my thighs.

"Is this okay?" she asks. "If I'm too heavy, I'll get the chair."

I put an arm around her, holding her tight against me. "You

are not too heavy at all." I lean in, inhaling deeply. Kef me, that scent of hers. "I want you to stay here forever."

"Might be awkward when someone visits," she teases, but she settles in a little closer, moving under my arm and then resting her head on my chest. No one has ever trusted me like this, and it makes me feel...things. A great many things. "Okay, so...where to begin."

I hold her a little tighter against me. "Wherever you like."

16

VICTOR

*B*ee thinks for a long moment. "So back home, I was a..." She pauses. "Well, I don't suppose it matters, but I was a project manager at a website designing firm. It wasn't what I wanted to do, but a bachelor's degree will only get you so far. Anyhow. I was working late one night in the office by myself. I had an overseas client that wanted to do a conference call, and so it was very late my time and early theirs. I'd done it before and didn't think anything of it. I guess it was around midnight when all the power in the building died, and when I went to the office window to see if there was a storm, I saw a flash of light and then the next thing I knew, I woke up...in space."

She swallows hard, loud enough that I can hear it, and her scent turns sour.

"Apparently," Bee continues, "humans are a hot commodity. I woke up and someone cuffed my hands and dragged me onto a stage at a slave auction. The man—alien, I guess—that bought me was older. He was very...unpleasant. He didn't care if I liked him touching me or not, and I didn't. Looking back, I kind of think that he deliberately bought someone that wouldn't like his touch because he got off on that." She swallows hard. "I think he had a wife back on Homeworld, because he kept me at his vacation house. At first I thought that was such a relief, because he would leave for long periods of time and I wouldn't have to endure him...but then his son started showing up. I guess he got Dad's permission to play with the toys."

There is a metallic tang to her scent now, and she is sweating. The memories are difficult for her. When she speaks, she hesitates repeatedly, as if she's having to force the words out. I think of pleasant, happy Bee, being hurt by these strangers, and it makes me want to destroy everything in reach.

Everything but her.

My grip on her must be tight, because she moves a little closer to me, as if trying to get away from it. When she sighs and presses her cheek against my chest, relaxing, I realize that I am wrong—she is seeking comfort from me. "That went on for five years," Bee says softly. "And I hated every day of it. I hated what they did to me, and I hated that they liked it when I cried. I hated that I was so powerless. I ran away once, to his neighbor, and asked for help. I begged him to help me find a safe place for humans, but instead, he just called my owner and demanded that he come get me."

"Are they still alive?" I growl. "Because I want to destroy all of them."

"Don't know, don't care," Bee says, and pats my chest with one of her small hands. "About a year and a half ago, the son abruptly gathered up all of my things and shoved me onto a spaceship. Didn't tell me what was going on, but I wonder if his mother found out about her husband's hideaway. Or maybe the neighbor complained. Either way, they got rid of me, and when

I got onto the spaceship and saw all the human women there, I thought I was going to be sold again. That my nightmare was starting over. Instead...it brought me here. And I was safe."

I squeeze her arm, and then I remember her bruises, and my temper flares all over again. "Not safe enough. Your skin is marked up."

"That's a recent development," Bee says, and her sigh is tired. "And it's partially my fault. I've never been attracted to Riffin. Actually I don't think I could ever be attracted to any of the mesakkah, not after what I went through. I'm sure there are some nice ones out there, but they just don't do anything for me. But this place...Lord va'Rin is trying to set it up as a haven for humans, but...sometimes we're just not safe no matter what. I think of it like a henhouse. Everyone is safe and happy until a fox sneaks in, and then no one's safe. I realize that doesn't mean anything to you." She pats my chest again. "But it's a perfect analogy for me. Sometimes a bad guy sneaks under the radar and then the humans aren't safe. So a lot of women have been marrying aliens to get a protector. I encouraged Riffin because I felt like I could control our relationship, and maybe with time, I could get used to the idea of him touching me. In a way, it was safe because it kept other men from approaching me."

"But he hurt you. And he made you kiss him and you did not want to."

She nods. "All true. Which is why we're done. I told him that, and I suspect he took it out on you. That's why your collar was turned on maximum 'accidentally.'" She lifts a hand and makes a gesture, crooking a finger. "Which is bullshit, and I'm furious that you were tortured. Furious." Her fists clench. "I know I told Novis I was going to keep quiet, but the more I think about it, the angrier I get. Riffin had no right—"

"It is done." I put a hand over her clenched fist. I love that she is angry on my behalf—it makes me feel good—but right now I am far more interested in getting her arousal scent in the air again than anything else. "You know what would make him furious?"

"What?" Bee sits up, facing me.

I grin, knowing full well that it makes my expression fearsome. "If we share breath and I make you come."

She tilts her head, studying me. "That *would* make him angry, yes. But the reason I told you all of this is because..." She clenches a fist over her heart. "The sexual part of me is dead inside. I don't want any sort of sexual relationship. At all. It does nothing for me."

"I understand...but I could make you come," I state again.

Bee's expression flicks with annoyance. "It's my body, and I know what it's capable of. Trust me, you can't."

"I bet I can. I am a champion. I am bred to be the best at all things. Why not pleasuring a female? Just because I have not done it yet doesn't mean that I cannot." When she looks away from me, I put a knuckle under her chin and gently guide her head up, forcing her to make eye contact with me. "I am a fast learner, Bee. Let me try."

She licks her lips, pulling away from me. "And when I stay dead inside?"

"You won't."

"Your arrogance is really irritating, you know that?"

"Arrogance? I see it as truth." I lean in, drinking in her scent. It's changing again, losing the fear-sourness and going back to her regular, pleasant one. She goes still when I move closer, her eyes fluttering shut, and I take that as a good sign. Carefully, I rub my nose against the soft skin at her temple, my hand curving to cup her thigh and holding her against me. "When we talk, your scent changes. I can smell your cunt growing wet when you are near me. Is that scent for me, or is it for one of the guards?"

She shudders when I mention the guards. "Not them."

"Then it is for me," I state, pleased. "And if my presence and my words can make your cunt wet, then surely the rest of me can." I want to rub my face all over her, to bathe in her scent. Kef, she smells so good I want to lick her all over. I drag one tusk through her soft mane, entranced by the scent of it. There's a hint of rain left there, and it just adds to the pleasure of breathing her in. I slide my hand up her back, and she feels so delicate under my grasp. I am clawed and fanged and spiked and dangerous, but she is in my embrace, her scent drifting towards arousal, and I enjoy this moment very, very much.

"Victor," Bee whispers.

"You like words," I murmur. "So we will start with words. Tell me how this sharing of breaths works. This kiss. Explain it to me."

Her breath hitches. "I could probably show you—"

"No, describe it first." I want to hear her say the words, to think about it, because I suspect if I just paw at her, I will be no better off than her mesakkah fool.

Bee's weight shifts on my leg. When she shifts again, I want to ask if she is uncomfortable, but then her arousal scent floods the room. She is squirming, restless, just like me. I bite back a groan of pleasure, keeping my expression neutral. If I tell her how much her scent has changed, she will skitter away, nervous. "Well," she begins, and her voice is husky and warm and delicious. She puts a hand on my chest and gazes at her fingers against my skin. "It is a human custom to show affection. You can kiss a friend or a relative on the cheek, but only lovers kiss on the mouth."

"Do lovers kiss anywhere else?" I ask, because my imagination is full of places I would like to put my mouth.

Bee's face flushes. She nods, her scent increases, and then she bats at my chest lightly. "You're getting ahead of me. We're describing mouth kisses."

"Very well. I shall be quiet so you may teach me."

Her brow goes up and she gives me a wry look. "You're not very good at being quiet."

I lean in. "So far, you are not very good at teaching."

A burst of nervous giggles escapes her, and Bee smiles. My heart feels as if it skips a beat in my chest, and I decide I like her smile even more than her arousal scent. I hunger for her, true, but...I want her to smile at me more than anything. All of the wet, perfumed cunts in the universe mean nothing if Bee is afraid of me. "You keep distracting me," Bee chides. "Hush if you want to learn."

"Consider me hushed."

That smile continues to play around her lips, and she tilts her head, thinking. Her fingers brush over my heart, and it takes everything I have to keep my tail from flicking in response to that light, pleasurable touch. My cock is hard and aching, but I ignore it. Right now, my entire focus is on Bee, and Bee's mouth. Bee's voice. "So when two people decide to take their relationship to the next level...they kiss." Her fingers trace small circles on my skin.

"Go on."

"You're really going to make me describe it, aren't you?"

"I really am." I am loving how she wriggles on my thigh, her expression consternated. "Please, go on."

Bee gives a gusty sigh, tapping a finger on my chest. "Okay, well...you move in close to one another, and you brush lips." She pauses, her gaze going to my mouth, and I wonder what she is thinking when she looks at it. It is not an attractive mouth, I know that. "Sometimes you just rub lips for a while. Or not really rubbing lips. It's more of a graze. A tease. A promise of what's to come. You're testing the waters, feeling each other out. So you press your mouth to the other person's in small, delicate brushes. You let the excitement build."

I remain silent, not wanting to interrupt. Her scent is every-where, her expression soft as she regards my face.

"Then at some point, one of you starts wanting more." Her voice is a mere whisper, her fingers like brands against my skin as she leans closer to me. Her breath fans against my skin, and our faces are near, but she does not close the gap between us. "You make the kiss a little deeper, a little more intense. You take things to the next level. You brush your tongue against the other person's lips, asking to be let in, and that's when it really becomes...special." She makes a breathless little sound. "Kisses are fine, but it's when you add in tongue that it really becomes pleasurable. It's like you're tasting the other person and teasing them at the same time. Not hard licks, of course. Soft, sensual licks. Slow licks that tell your partner what you'd be like in bed together. A sensual lick that promises other good licks." Her lashes flutter and her gaze goes to my mouth again, her fingers tracing the lines of my pectoral. "Maybe that's not what other people think of when they kiss, but I do. It's about giving pleasure to your partner. Making sure that with every flick of your tongue, every brush of your lips, you're making sure that they're enjoying themselves as much as you are. It's almost like a dance. And if one partner is clumsy, it can ruin everything."

"I would not be clumsy," I promise her. Isn't that what I have wanted all along? To watch and see what pleasures her and repeat that? "So the tongue in the mouth...this is how you come?"

Bee's startled gaze goes to my eyes. "What? N-no, you need more stimulation for that."

"So...two tongues," I say gravely, keeping my face bland.

She sputters. "Two tongues? No! I mean—" She smacks my chest with a light hand, realizing I am teasing her. "You're ridiculous, you know that?"

"Three tongues, then?"

Her choked laughter is followed by another charming smack on my skin. Her hand is so small, the slap so light that it is nothing more than a tickle, but I like that she feels free enough to touch my bare skin as she likes. "Here I am trying to be serious," she says with a chuckle, "and you're mocking me."

"Not mocking. Just trying to figure out the best way to pleasure you." I smile at her, stroking my hand up and down her back, just because she feels so good in my arms. "What if I have one big tongue instead of many tongues, but I promise to lick you well?"

Bee's breathing stutters, and her gaze flicks to my mouth again. Suddenly all of my teasing disappears, and I want nothing more than to kiss her and taste her. To tease her with my tongue like she said. She licks her lips, and I wonder if my mouth is revolting to her. Her teeth are small and square. Mine are dangerous and sharp, with the ever-present tusks that jut out of my lower jaw and curve up to dig into my cheek. Her lips are soft-looking and dusky pink, and mine are...not.

I want to ask her to kiss me, but I cannot form the words. I need her to suggest it, or else I am no better than Crulden the Ruiner.

Her hand steals up from my chest and she caresses my cheek. I close my eyes, savoring that small touch. I'm starved for it. I need her to touch me constantly, because it reminds me that she's here and I'm not alone or surrounded by enemies. That someone in this universe thinks I am more than just a cloned asshole.

"Do you want your prize?" Bee whispers, her thumb stroking along my jaw. "My champion?"

My cock surges and I bite back a groan as it presses against my too-tight trou. I force myself to open my eyes, and Bee is looking up, her beautiful face turned toward me. "You want to kiss me?"

"I think so...but I might feel nothing," she adds hastily. "So please understand if I don't like it." Her worried gaze searches my face. "It's just...it's not you..."

"You will like it," I reassure her. "Do not fret."

Her mouth quirks at my confidence, and then her gaze goes to my mouth again. I watch her consider, and then she cups my face with both of her hands, studying my lips. I remain completely still, letting her examine my face. I know we will not be able to kiss as normal, but I know I can still make it enjoyable for her, because for me, it will be all about her pleasure.

Bee's mouth brushes lightly over my top lip, between my tusks. It is a soft, ticklish sensation, made all the better by her breath fanning against mine. I love the scent of her, and it only grows as she presses another tender kiss against my upper lip. I let her explore me, keeping still as her mouth goes to my lower lip and she kisses it, too. The brush of lips is nice enough, but I can see what she meant by needing more stimulation than this to come.

Then, she gently bites down on my lower lip and sucks on it.

I suck in a breath, the sound startled and strange to my own ears. Bee immediately pulls back, a worried expression on her face. "That was bad?"

"You...did not tell me there would be biting."

"Oh." Bee pauses. "I mean, there is some gentle biting if you are in the moment, but if you don't like it, I can stop—"

I put a careful finger to her lips before she can finish that statement. "I like it. I like it very much."

Bee smiles and licks the pad of my finger, and the feel of her tongue goes straight to my cock.

This time, I cannot bite back my groan. This is supposed to be about me pleasuring her, and she is distracting me. I need to turn this around on her. "Can I try it? On you?"

"Of course."

I slide my hand over her backside and then up her spine. Bee squirms a little again, and it's clear I've surprised her by starting with a touch. I run my hand over her shoulders, studying her as I move along her skin. I'm careful not to adjust the blanket she has wrapped around her body, since she told me that was off limits. I'm careful with my claws, tracing the pads of my fingers over her flesh since one wrong move will slice her open. She has a fascinating little dip at the base of her throat where I can practically see her pulse, and I lightly brush my finger over it. "Is there something in particular you like? If not kissing?"

She turns confused, slightly distracted eyes to me. "I didn't say I don't like kissing."

"I have seen you kiss this mesakkah fool. You said it did nothing for you. So I am asking what you do like. Have you an idea?" When she shakes her head, I offer, "Biting? Does he bite your lip?" I feel obvious asking that, because the biting was my favorite thing so far. "Or is he a licker?"

She wrinkles her nose. "Ugh, let's not call him a licker. Kissing him is...unpleasant. I just don't like his mouth. Do we have to talk about him?"

"I am thinking of ways to pleasure you, that is all. I want my kiss to be the champion kiss."

That makes her chuckle. "I'm sure it will be."

But she does not know, and I have not even started yet. So I stroke up her neck, and when she shivers, I realize this is another thing she did not mention, just like the biting—that she likes touches. That she likes being stroked and petted. I make note of this, and I am starting to realize that there is more to kissing than just mouths and tongues.

I cup her face in my hands, drinking in the sight of her. I have waited a long, long time to be able to touch her, and now that I can, having her in my arms is like a dream. I want to do this right. I want to do everything right. I lean in to kiss her... and bump my large nose against her smaller one.

A smile spreads across Bee's pretty face. "I forgot to warn you about noses."

"Noses," I murmur. "And biting. You seem to have left out a great many things."

Her chuckle warms me. "It's just...one of those sorts of things that you do on instinct more than anything else."

My instincts are full of destruction, though. Of someone else's memories. I cannot trust them at all. So I remind myself of all the things once more—noses, biting, touches—and then lean in and carefully, carefully place my lips over hers. Her taste sings through my senses, but most of all, I am acutely aware of her skin pressing against mine, of her teats pushing against my chest as I cup her face and kiss her, and of the feel of her against me. I rub my lips gently against hers, mimicking her actions and studying her responses.

She is quiet, her pulse calm as I push my mouth against hers, so I try something else. As she did to me, I nip at her lower lip, taking it into my mouth and sucking on it. That causes a burst of her arousal to scent the air, and between tasting her and that scent, I nearly forget my plan of attack. Instead, I luxuriate in Bee's closeness, her skin, her scent, her mouth, and nibble on her lips over and over again, until I release her lip and swipe my tongue over her top one.

That makes her gasp, her hands clenching against my chest. She lets out a small, shuddering breath, and squirms on my thigh again.

"May I tongue you?" I murmur, even though I have done it once already and she liked it. Bee likes control, so I will give her as much as I can...or the illusion of it, anyhow.

My words make her shiver, but she nods against my hands, her eyes heavy-lidded and dazed as she gazes up at me.

I lean in, careful to do this right, and think that this Riffin is a fool. Bee's cunt smells so beautifully that it is making my mouth water. How did he fail to pay attention to her small signals? She does not know how to ask for pleasure—is not even sure she wants to ask—but she still enjoys it. I tilt my head, careful to slant my mouth over hers the way she showed me, and slick my tongue into her mouth again.

Later, when I have time to go over every detail, I will revel in her taste and how her mouth feels. For now, it is all about Bee and her responses. How I can make her cunt wet and dripping with need. How I can make her squirm on my leg until she is panting aloud and clinging to me, demanding more kisses.

I stroke my tongue against hers experimentally. Mine feels so much larger than hers that I worry about choking her with my enthusiasm. I keep my movements light and teasing, dipping my tongue against hers in toying motions that promise more without overwhelming. Her taste and scent are everywhere, and when she makes a soft, whimpering sound against my conquering mouth, I want to shout to the skies with triumph.

I *am* a champion kisser, after all.

17

BEE

I lie on the narrow bed that night and touch my mouth, my thoughts whirling.

It didn't take long for Victor to make a liar out of me. Jesus. That kiss was...intense. Actually I don't even know if I can call it a kiss, because it was more of a make-out session and the kissing was just an afterthought. It was like he was utterly focused on my pleasure, on how to use his tongue on me. His hands were everywhere, and he touched me and studied me so thoroughly that I was practically flinging myself at him by the time he finally truly tongue-kissed me.

It was...intense. Achingly sweet, oh-so-careful, and so good that hours later I'm still thinking about it.

I squeeze my thighs together in the bed, because my pulse is pounding between them. I'm clothed now, but that doesn't stop the barrage of emotions racing through me. I might as well be naked and touching myself, because I don't think I could be any more turned on. After we broke apart from the kiss, I babbled a million excuses as to why I needed to escape, and practically flung myself off his lap and raced away to the far end of the house. I'm pretty sure if Victor could purr, he'd be purring in that moment. I've never seen a guy look so damn satisfied with himself.

I'm also pretty sure he could smell how turned on I was. He smells everything.

So I spent the rest of the evening racing around the house, putting things away, drying our clothes (mine first) and then making a list of things we needed. Victor needs more clothes, I need more clothes, we need food, a bed for him...the list goes on and on.

As if he sensed I needed space, Victor kept to himself, poking around at the house and the grounds, checking out everything possible. I blushed all through our protein bar dinner, and after that, feigned tiredness. He insisted I take the bed and I did, but I've been laying here for hours, unable to sleep. There's no blanket to curl up in—the pillow's still on Victor's "chair" and since he can't take the bed, I insisted he take the blanket. I feel guilty that I'm the one with the comfortable spot, but the truth is, I'm not that comfortable at all.

I'm restless, and for what might be the first time in years, I'm completely and utterly horny and I don't know what to do with that. I put a hand on my belly and then move it lower, testing the waters. It feels good and none of the awful memories surface, so I move a bit lower, cupping my mound through my pants.

A new thought occurs to me—if I touch myself, is Victor going to hear me get off?

As if burned, I snatch my hand away. I turn on my side, tuck an arm under my head, and stare at the wall as I try to go to sleep.

NEW, fresh guilt surges through me when I wake up in the morning to find Victor curled up on the hard floor. It looks uncomfortable, but one of his spikes has already pierced through the blanket, and I remind myself that if he destroys all of our furniture, we'll be worse off. Still, it's hard. I want him to have nice things, and that includes a real chair and a bed. I move to the comm unit and quietly whisper my list of things so Herrix and Akris can acquire them, and I emphasize that we need them today. When I'm done, I turn around and Victor is watching me, his eyes heavy, relaxed slits.

"Did I wake you? I'm sorry. I can't send them a written list. They don't read English and I don't read Homeworld." I give him a cheery smile. "Want breakfast?"

"You smell good," he says, a languid note in his voice.

A hot blush creeps through me. So much for keeping things at a "friend" level. We both know what he's referring to when he mentions my scent. I decide to ignore it, turning towards the counters and where I put away the food. "I can fire something up in the processor, or we can eat more protein bars. I'm not a huge fan of the food supplies that they gave us, so I've asked the guards to bring in some other options. You've probably got a fierce metabolism and need a lot of food." My senses prick as I pick up a mug, and when I turn around, he gets to his feet and stretches, all feline grace despite the spikes and claws. He stalks toward me and I clutch the mug against my chest. "If there's anything in particular you want to eat, just let me know..."

Victor sidles toward me, and there's a hungry look in his eyes as he places one big hand on the counter behind me, leaning in. "I've thought of my new prize."

I stare up at him, flustered by his nearness. I keep thinking about how he'd kissed me last night, as if my pleasure was the only thing important to him. How he'd cupped my face and tasted my mouth so sweetly, and how he'd run his hands all over my body just because he liked touching me. I'd throbbed with awareness last night, and it had taken forever for me to fall asleep. That awareness is back this morning, curling through me and making everything in my body race. "New...prize?"

He nods. "A champion must have a prize, after all."

"Right. Of course." It's hard for me to think when he's so close. When he looks so smugly satisfied with himself. It's the same smug expression he was wearing last night after we kissed, when I knew he could smell just how turned on I was. That arousal is flaring through me again, as I imagine what his next demand is. "W-what did you have in mind?"

"I am thinking...more immediate goals." His other hand goes to the counter, and I'm neatly trapped under him.

Is he going to demand a kiss right now? Because...I don't think I'd hate that. Not in the slightest.

"Every day of good behavior, of learning and obeying these rules of society, I will want my prize. A kiss every night." He gives me another self-satisfied smile. "What do you say to that?"

Part of me is a little disappointed he's not asking for more than a kiss, but that's my imagination racing away with me. Even so, a daily kiss is going to be...a lot. It'll mean sitting on his lap every night and tonguing each other and his hands all over me and I'm getting turned on just thinking about it. "I think that's manageable." I glance toward the door, biting my lip. "We should probably keep it secret from the guards though. If they think I'm here with you just for kissing, they might separate us and give you a new teacher."

His nostrils flare, his tail lashing behind him like an angry cat. "Let them try. I will make them regret it."

"You're supposed to be working on becoming civilized," I remind him. "That's not a very civilized thing to say."

"That's because I don't care if I'm civilized or not." Victor leans in, looming over me in a way that makes me want to squirm with heat. "I'm only in this for the kisses."

I should be upset at that confession. I want him to do this

for himself. But at the same time...I'm not exactly upset about the kissing part of the bargain myself.

Victor leans in, and for a moment, I think he's going to start the day with a kiss—only to have him jerk away, staring at the walls of the house. A look of boyish delight crosses his face. "It's raining again."

I bite back a smile, because he looks so thrilled at that realization. "When it rains here, it tends to rain for a few days, yeah." I watch his expression. "You like the rain?"

"It smells so good. And I like the feel of it on my skin. It feels...clean."

I get it. For a man who's been cooped up in a cell ever since he awoke, rain must be fresh and new to him. "We'll probably have to turn the wheels on the pump house again."

He heads for the door. "I can do that right now—"

Before he can move away, I grab his hand. Victor looks down at me as I squeeze his fingers. "You should eat breakfast first."

AFTER WE EAT A VERY uninspiring meal, Victor heads outside to the pump house. I hear a low, metallic grinding noise that tells me he's turning the crank, and then it sounds like a toilet flushing. I guess that's the water being sucked away. It's something I'm going to have to get used to if the pump house needs to be utilized regularly. I check in on Victor after I clean up the kitchen, and he's still at work inside the small pump house, cleaning and oiling the gears with a determined look on his face. The floor is mucky with mud, and I immediately start sneezing and retreat inside.

Overall it's a quiet day. Victor obsesses with cleaning the pump house and the stone walkway that's more or less been covered with mud at this point. He scrapes the packed down mud off flagstones, revealing a pretty path connecting the house to the pumps. I think he likes being outdoors, and the rain doesn't bother him, so I let him work there all day. We can always do more practical lessons later tonight. Maybe I should show him how to make meals for himself, or how to use the comm panels.

Akris comes by late afternoon with a large bag of things I've requested. There's still no new mattress for Victor or a chair. Those are being printed in town and will be delivered tomorrow. I'm a little disappointed, but at least there are extra blankets and towels now, along with some spices to make the bland foodstuffs we've been given a bit more exciting. There's also a package of meat, because I know Victor likes meat, and I want to give him things that make him happy. I want to show him that there are good things in the universe that don't have to be bargained for. That sometimes, all you have to do is ask.

More than that, I need him to realize that not all the guards are like Riffin and Novis. Some are married to their jobs, true, but a lot are just young alien men with their first posting away from home, doing a job. It's not that Victor's the enemy. He's a job. The sooner he realizes that, the sooner he can make friends and maybe realize that even though we've been thrown into the deep end of the pool, so to speak, we can still swim.

I set out all the ingredients for dinner, so Victor can make it. I rearrange what little furniture we have so we can sit together (though a small, naughty part of me thinks I should leave it as it is so I have to sit on his lap again). I wait by the table, drumming my fingers while I wait for him to come in. Not for the first time, I wish I had a book to read. There's a few treasured books back in Port that have been scraped together, but it seems selfish to ask for one when there's such a demand for them.

The door opens.

I sit up as Victor enters, soaked to the bone and covered in mud. But his grin is wide with satisfaction. "I have uncovered the entire path."

"That's wonderful," I say, and then promptly sneeze.

His expression immediately changes to concern. "Why are you sneezing? You didn't go outside."

I rub my nose. "Allergies. It's the dirt."

Victor glances down at his muddy legs and trou, and at the trail of mud he's dragged into the house. He's not wearing shoes, probably because those lethal toe-claws of his won't fit in any mesakkah or human shoe, and it's just made the mess worse. He frowns down at his appearance. "This is bad, then. I need to clean off."

I sneeze again, hating that my nose is filling up. I wave a hand at the bathroom. "Go shower off. I'll clean the floors."

He heads into the lavatory and shuts the door behind him, and I program one of the cleaner bots to take care of the mess. I blow my nose twice, wipe my watering eyes while the bot merrily spins a path on the floor, getting rid of the mud. It takes me a minute to realize that the lavatory is silent. There's no sound of running water.

Well that's not good. I hop off the countertop and move to the door, knocking. "Everything all right in there?"

There's a long pause and then a grunt. "I do not know how this device works."

Did he not shower before? The controls are standard. Then I curse myself for being an assuming asshole. He was kept caged for the first weeks of his awakening, and when he was freed, his cell didn't have a shower hookup. I'm such an ass. "That can be today's lesson, then. I'll show you how to work everything in the lavatory. Let me in?"

He opens the door and I step inside—

And pause.

Why did it not occur to me that Victor would be naked when

I came in? Because he's absolutely stark naked right now, and my gaze goes to the enormous cock hanging between his legs. Even flaccid, it's thicker than it has any right to be. The tip is bulbous and flushed, and the velvety undercoat that covers all of his skin seems to be nonexistent near his groin, which is the darker tan of his bared skin. He's completely swallowed by his foreskin, and underneath it, it looks like he's covered in tiny, textured bumps.

Oh.

As I stare, his cock stiffens, rising proudly in response to my gaze. The shaft thickens, and Victor's breath speeds up.

"Shower time," I call cheerfully, dragging my gaze away from the sight of his cock. It's not polite to stare, not polite to ask to take a closer look, certainly not polite to ask to watch as his foreskin retreats down his shaft, revealing the rest of him to my greedy, fascinated gaze. "You can get clean and I can stop sneezing."

"You were looking at my cock," Victor murmurs as I brush past him. Oh mercy, just the simple act of moving toward the shower is distracting, as I can feel the hot prod of him against my body when I move past. "I saw you looking," he prompts. "Admit it, Bee."

He's not going to let me get away with hiding under the guise of politeness, is he? I bite the inside of my cheek, wanting to shriek in frustration at how conflicted I feel. Part of me wants to turn around and grab that thick length and stop pussy-footing around the situation. The other part of me wants to race out the bathroom door and never return.

But I've promised to be his teacher, so I ignore his question and put on my managing smile. "Here, step inside the shower booth and I'll show you how the controls work."

"Why will you not answer me?" Victor prompts. "Is my cock misshapen?"

"It's a very nice cock," I manage, staring desperately at the control panels to the shower. "But we're not talking about this right now, Victor. I'm here to show you—"

"You liked the sight of it," he continues. "I can smell your arousal. It's starting. You approve of my naked body." He sounds pleased. "Can I see yours?"

"We're not doing this right now," I say again, my tone sharper.

"Why not?"

I dare a look over my shoulder, keeping my gaze focused purely on his face. "Because I've told you how I feel about sexuality. I'll kiss you but I don't want to take it further than that."

"Bee, I do not understand. I have proven that you can still feel desire. I did last night with my kiss, and I am right now with my pleasing form. I like it when you look at me. What is the harm in that?"

"There's no harm in looking, but it never stops at just looking," I point out. "Guys always want more."

He's silent. Then, "I would not ask you to touch me."

Now I feel like the bad guy after hearing that somber, almost sad note in his voice. Is he daring me to prove that I find him attractive? "I agreed to kisses," I begin again. "Not—"

"I would not ask you to touch me," he states again. "It is all right, Bee. I merely wanted you to look because it makes me feel good. That is as far as it can go."

I'm so very confused by this conversation. I turn around and frown up at his face. He's no longer smiling and cocky, the "champion" as he likes to proclaim himself. If anything, his expression is downright unhappy. "You're confusing me, Victor."

"Bee," he says, and his voice is low and gentle. His expression is still vaguely sad, as if something amazing has been dangled in his reach and then snatched away again. "There is nothing I would like more than your hands upon my cock, but I would never ask for such a thing. I cannot."

I lick my lips, keeping my gaze glued to his. I'm not going to look down at his massive body or tight hips or the cock that feels as if it's taking up all the space in between us. "Because... it'll make you lose control?"

He shakes his head. "Because it'll hurt you."

Hurt me? I fight the urge to roll my eyes. I mean, he's a big boy, but it's not as if I couldn't handle that sort of thing. I steal a quick look down, and as I do, he runs one finger along his shaft, from tip to base.

And I really look at him. Those bumps under his foreskin were not bumps at all. They're spines, covering the shaft of his cock. They all face in one direction, and I come to the realization that if he pushed into me, it'd feel great. Coming out, however...

My eyes go wide. I stare up at him, at his sad, wry expression. "Look only," he says. "You are too soft to do more than look. That is why I only ask for kisses, Bee."

"You have barbs on your cock," I point out, stunned. Of all the things I expected him to be referring to, this certainly wasn't it.

"I do." He grips his shaft, squeezing. "But it doesn't mean you cannot look."

When he starts to move his hand, pumping to pleasure himself, I grab his wrist. "What are you doing? You're going to hurt yourself."

He huffs, the sound more amused than pained. "Maybe I like it when you stare."

I squeeze his wrist, indicating he should let go, and when he lifts his hand, it's bleeding. I flip it over, brushing a finger over his torn palm, and realization hits me. I look up at him. "Oh, Victor. Is this what you were doing? When you were self-harming?"

He shrugs, but that hint of amusement is on his face. "It was worth it."

I make a sound of pure frustration. This man is impossible. "You're not allowed to masturbate if you hurt yourself in the process. I won't allow it."

"Because you don't like me touching myself?"

"Because I don't like you hurting yourself, you stubborn ass!"

"Asshole," he corrects, and gives me another toothy grin. "The guards say I am 'asshole,' remember?"

I am going to start screaming in frustration in a minute. This man—this alien—is impossible. Fine. He wants me to use words he'll understand, I'll use them. "If you touch yourself like that, it makes my cunt dry up, all right? It makes me not want to kiss you because it'll lead to you hurting yourself, and that displeases me more than anything."

Victor's amused expression disappears. "Fair," he says, his tone almost sulky. He drops his hands to his sides and nods at the shower. "Show me how to clean myself, then."

18

BEE

*M*y fuming only lasts through his shower. I'm getting mad at the wrong things, I realize. I shouldn't be mad at Victor for touching himself and taking comfort in the only thing he can. I should be mad that he was put into an untenable situation with nothing but misery around him. I should be mad that whoever modified him fucked up his body with spikes and tusks and now goddamn penis barbs.

I also come to the realization that I'm mad because he's made me feel things that I haven't wanted in forever, and now that I'm starting to want them again, I can't have them.

But that isn't Victor's fault, either.

He opens the lavatory door and sticks his head out. "I am getting water everywhere, Bee. How do I make it stop?"

I jump to my feet. "Use a towel to mop yourself dry? Wrap it around your body?"

Victor shakes his head. "And destroy it? We just got it."

Good point. "You can towel off and avoid your spikes, maybe."

"How?"

My face heats at the thought of me showing him how to towel off, but I remind myself that this is just another thing he's unfamiliar with. How can I possibly expect him to know how to practice good hygiene if he's never been given a chance? "All right, I'll show you."

He steps back from the door and I join him in the lavatory. It looks like a damned car crash in the shower, with mud and fur everywhere, but I ignore that. The moment I step inside, the bathroom is practically being swallowed up by Victor's big, hulking body. A big, hulking, wet body.

And he's still got suds in his hair.

I really am the worst teacher. Frustrated with myself, I move back to the edge of the shower and tap the control panel. "You need to rinse everything off, Victor. Even the shampoo."

"Shampoo?"

"The bottle? Did you use the bottle?"

"You showed me soap." He points at the dispenser in the wall. "I used soap."

I wrinkle my nose. "You don't use that on your hair. I mean, I guess you could. Shampoo and conditioner will make it soft, though. Those are human things." I point at the bottles tucked on one of the built-in shelves on the wall. They were included in the trunk as part of the "human welcome package," which I suspect is courtesy of Lord va'Rin's human wife. I reach over the shower, plucking one of the bottles from its spot. "You wet your hair. You put a small amount of this in your hair. Then you rinse it out. Then you put a small amount of the other bottle in your hair. Then you rinse it out."

He sniffs the bottle, his big nose flaring. "It seems like a lot of work."

This is worse than a toddler. "It'll make your hair nice and soft and shiny."

His gaze goes to me. "And you like this?"

"I do."

He grumbles, but steps into the shower again. "Will you watch to make sure I do it correctly? I do not like being wrong."

It probably doesn't fit with his champion mentality. I nod, picking up the discarded towel and holding it as he steps under the spray again. Water sluices down his big body, and when he lifts his arms to wash his hair, it makes his torso look long and sleek...and his cock obscenely prominent.

And because I'm a mess around this guy, I can't stop looking at him. He's glorious like this. I mean, he's glorious most of the time, but wet and slick and aroused? He looks incredible and I can feel my body responding to the sight of him.

He goes through everything I explained, and when he finally shuts the water off, his normally fluffy, wild mane of hair is plastered against his skull. His triangular ears stick out and his expression is slightly distrusting as I hold the towel out to him. Victor takes it from me and dabs lightly at his chest, his frown increasing.

I bite back a giggle at the sight. "It's going to take you all day if you do it like that."

"Then show me." Victor holds the towel in my direction.

It's totally a challenge. A dare. He wants to see how I react. If I shy away from his hard cock or if I'm going to pat him down and dry him off.

I take the towel and remind myself that I'm his teacher. That's why I want to do this. It's not for any other, purely selfish, purely physical reason. It's certainly not because I want to touch him. It's because he needs drying off. It's so he doesn't drip water all over the floors. It's so he doesn't catch a cold...

Oh, who am I kidding? He's gorgeous and naked and right in front of me and I can't resist.

I take a daring step forward, and I'm eye level with his abdomen and pectorals. If I was a taller human woman, we might have a more equivalent height. Since I'm a short bit of fluff, it puts me that much closer to his cock. His thorny, thorny cock. I step forward to dry him and it practically stabs me in the boobs. And because I'm not immune to him like I think I am, I glance down.

There's a big, fat bead of pre-cum glazing the tip. As I watch, it slides down that thick, prominent crown and drips down the underside.

"Maybe...maybe I should start with your back," I breathe. "Turn around for me?"

Victor does as I ask, bracing his hands on the tiles of the shower. This isn't much better, because from this view, I get a good look at his tight, rounded buttocks and firm thighs. The spikes, too, but I somehow seem to notice them less as time goes by. I'm more interested in the man underneath all the armor, the one who wears the cocky grin of a champion but who won't let me touch his cock because he's afraid he'll hurt me.

As if the only thing to sex is putting a cock inside a vagina.

I carefully towel him dry, avoiding the lethal-looking spikes that go up and down his shoulders and the backs of his arms and down the sides of his back. They disappear at his buttocks and re-appear again below the knee, so I focus on drying the parts of him that are easiest to reach before dropping to a crouch to get his legs.

Victor groans, his claws screeching against the tile.

I freeze, jumping up in alarm. He looks over at me, but his eyes aren't red. They're hooded with arousal, full of hungry need, and I realize my toweling is only making it worse. Touching him is turning me on, too, and between my touch and my scent, I'm probably making him crazy.

"I need to touch myself," he rasps. His cock twitches, and another bead of pre-cum appears. "Leave me, Bee."

I shake my head. I've come to a brand new realization just now.

I want Victor...and I want to show him that we can do more than just kiss. I want to make him feel good. I want to make him feel like a normal man, not the monster he imagines himself. So I continue toweling his legs off. "Don't scratch up the tile or I'll be sad."

He groans again, louder. "Bee—"

"I'm almost done, Victor," I say softly. "And then we're going to kiss. And after that, we'll have dinner. Unless you're starving?"

"Kiss." He grits the word out, hoarse. "I want to kiss."

"Me too," I admit, moving the drying towel along his other leg carefully and when they're dry enough, I move to his stomach and pat it down. He's still got his hands braced on the wall, which means I get under him, just a little, and...okay, I'm teasing him just because it turns me on. "Lean down so I can towel your hair for you."

He doesn't, of course. Victor is stubborn and likes to have the upper hand. Instead, he grabs me by the waist and hauls me into the air, setting me down atop the countertop. I stand over the sink, feeling incredibly tall and just a little bit afraid of heights, but that fear disappears when he straightens and then his mane is at chest level. His hands go to my waist, holding me in place, and I begin to towel off his hair. He groans, closing his eyes as I rub him down. "Feels good."

That makes me smile. "It's nice to have someone fuss over you, isn't it?"

His mouth curves in a faint hint of a smile of his own. He doesn't open his eyes, but I get the idea that he's focused on me anyhow. "Who fusses over you, Bee?"

"No one, and you already know that," I chide him, rubbing

his hair vigorously. He's got a ton of it on his head, just like a lion mane, and it's thick and textured and rather wild. I wonder if he should comb it out, because I don't know if it normally tangles. I toy with a strand and then scratch my nails over his scalp. "Feel better?"

Victor groans and buries his face against my belly. "Amazing," he murmurs. "I feel amazing. Will you touch me every time I shower?"

I wriggle in his grip, because the top of his head is pressing against the undersides of my breasts, and I'm very aware of his face as he nuzzles against my stomach. "You don't want to wash yourself?"

"Kef no. Want you to do it." He drags his tusks against my tunic. "You and your soft little human hands."

I let out a whimper, because he makes that sound so sexy. Like bathing is the most erotic thing possible.

Victor lifts his head, and as he does, his gaze goes to my breasts. "Your clothes are wet."

I glance down, distracted. Sure enough, his mane and skin have dampened the thin fabric of my tunic, and it sticks to my body. My nipples are tight and visible even through the band of fabric I wear as a bra. His eyes lock on them, and reverently, he reaches up and brushes a fingertip over one nipple.

I gasp, arousal flooding through me with dizzying speed. "Victor."

He makes a purring sound of pleasure, gliding his fingertip over the aching tip, and his claw catches on the fabric, tearing a small hole. Victor frowns, and when he lifts his hand, I realize he's gazing at his claws. His nostrils flare, and a look of self-loathing crosses his face as he releases me. "I want these gone, Bee. I want to be able to touch you and not be afraid that I'm going to spear you somehow."

"Okay," I say softly, and put my arms out. "Help me down and we can take care of that."

He pulls on a pair of trou, and for the next while, I clip his claws down as short as I can and then file the rough edges. I work on his toes, too, squaring down his nails so they look a bit more like mine. I'm not a hundred percent sure how alien nails are supposed to look, but he seems pleased with the results. When I'm done, he lifts one finger, scratches at the sleeve of my tunic, and grins when the fabric doesn't tear.

"Perfect," he says, and immediately hauls me into his arms.

I squeak as he lifts me into the air, my breasts over his shoulder. I cling to his head so I don't lose my balance. "Victor! Put me down!"

"Soon," he promises. "I want my kiss."

He carries me into the living area of the small house, heading for his seat with the pillow. When he sits, he pulls me into his lap, settling me on his thigh. One big hand goes to my backside and he tugs me in close, pulling me against his chest. His eyes are bright as they search my face, and he must like what he sees, because that faint purr starts up again. "May I kiss you now?"

Breathless, I nod.

Part of me expects him to cup my face again, but he hauls me up by my bottom and plasters me against his chest. I adjust my legs, sliding them over his hips until I'm straddling his big body. I'm panting with excitement when he drags me up against him and presses his mouth to mine. It's a light, chaste kiss at first, as if testing the waters. But I'm just as eager for more as he is, and I slide my hands to his neck, holding on to him as I open my lips in silent invitation. The next time he kisses me, it's with fierce abandon, his tongue brushing against mine. His mouth meets mine, tasting and teasing with every flick of his tongue, until I'm practically rubbing myself against his chest as we kiss, letting the friction work magic on my nipples.

Victor kisses as if he's a dying man and I'm his last breath.

He kisses me with such fierce intensity that I forget everything but the next brush of his mouth over mine, the next dip of his tongue against mine. I've never craved a kiss like I crave his, and it's all because he makes me feel like I'm the only thing in the world that matters. That I'm the most desirable creature he's ever seen, and he'll die if he doesn't have more of me in the next moment.

"You smell so keffing good, Bee," he growls between kisses. He grips my hips and drags me over his clothed cock. "I want to touch you all over. I want my mouth all over this soft little body of yours."

I whimper, because the hard bulge of his cock feels good between my legs, and yet I know it's dangerous. Terribly, terribly dangerous. I know I can't have what I want, but it doesn't mean we can't enjoy ourselves. So I kiss him again, showing him all of the excitement I'm feeling, and then pull back. "Victor...can I touch you?"

He pulls back, giving me a curious look. "You are touching me."

I shake my head, because he's not understanding. I reach down between us and run my thumb over the head of his cock.

The breath hisses out from between his teeth. "Bee." My name is a ragged syllable on his lips. "You shouldn't—"

"We can touch a little," I promise him. "Carefully." I stroke a hand down his chest and then graze the head of his cock again. "Do you trust me enough to let me make you come?"

He hauls me up against him again, startling me, and then he's pressing his mouth to mine again. It's more tusk than lip, but I can feel his big body trembling slightly under mine. It's like his need is so great he doesn't know how to express it, and it melts my heart.

We kiss again, and I nip at his lower lip, then soothe it with my tongue. "I'll make you feel so good, I promise."

"I'm yours, Bee." His gaze is intense as he watches me, so full of hunger that it makes my pussy clench. No one has ever looked at me like that. Like I could destroy him with a breath. "But only if you want to."

"Oh, I want to," I promise him. "Can't you smell how much I want it?"

He groans, his eyes wide, and gives me a jerky nod. "Keffing love your smell," he grits out. "So good."

My pussy clenches again, and I'm so wet that when I shift my weight, I can feel the slickness of my folds brush against each other. I haven't been this wet in god knows how long, and it feels good. It feels...powerful, for a change. I'm in control, and I'm bringing this terrifying, fierce man to his knees with the promise of a touch.

God, I love it.

With a little wriggle, I slide off his lap entirely and get to my feet. Victor starts to get up after me, clearly not grasping what I plan on doing, and I put a hand on his chest. "You stay right there. Relax. Let me take care of you again." I step between his thighs and slide my arms around his neck, then give him a teasing, nipping kiss. "Let me make you feel good."

"Bee," he groans, clearly at the end of his rope...or so he thinks.

Sweet man. He really has no idea.

I continue to kiss him, even as I reach down and rub the bulge of his cock. I do so with light, gentle fingers, because I don't want those barbs hurting him, but he seems to enjoy my touch. I feather my fingertips over his length, from tip to sac, and because he's so big, I can't kiss his mouth all the way through it. I make sure I'm kissing his chest or neck, though, because I can't get enough of him.

"Bee," he calls again, reaching for me. His hand moves over my shoulder, then cups one of my breasts through the fabric of my tunic. "Bee, let me touch you—"

"You are," I promise him. I want this to be about him

feeling good. About him realizing that just because he's got, well, barbs, it doesn't mean he's not worthy of being touched. He's made me feel so many things that I thought were dead inside me. I absolutely want to make him come, and I'm going to do whatever I can so he doesn't feel like he's missing out.

So I undo the fastener on his trou and pull the fabric down, careful to avoid his barbs. He looks just as rigid and enormous as I remember, and the head of his cock is wet with pre-cum. His sac is tight between his thighs, and I trace a finger over it. His skin is incredibly soft here, but when his tail twitches, I back off in case it's too much. I concentrate on the head of his cock instead, drawing teasing circles in the slickness there and rubbing it over and over again. I settle one hand on his chest, over his nipple, and brush it with my thumb as I tilt my face up towards his for a kiss.

He cups my face, groaning, and practically devours my mouth. "You..." he manages. "Bee..."

"Tell me to stop if something doesn't feel good," I say between urgent kisses. He bites at my lip, his big body straining under me, and I move my fingers faster, teasing his nipple and the tip of his cock with quicker motions.

Victor's fingers curl against my neck and he closes his eyes, his mouth against mine. Not kissing—he's too distracted. His hips jerk and the head of his cock bobs against my fingers, as if he's desperately trying to stop himself from pumping into my grip.

"Let go," I whisper against his lips, rubbing the head of his cock. "Let go."

"Need..."

"More?" I prompt, understanding. "If I give you more, do you promise not to move?" And I squeeze the head of his cock with a circle of my fingers.

He nods frantically, the look in his eyes desperate with

hunger. I kiss him one more time and then slide my hand lower. "Don't move," I remind him. "You can come, but don't move."

And I wrap my hand around his barbed length and squeeze.

It doesn't hurt—the barbs are angled backward, so just pressing my hand against his length doesn't drive them into my skin. But it changes everything for Victor. He lets out a muffled gasp, his head falling back against the wall. His hands dig into the trunk he's seated upon, but without his claws, there's nothing to hold onto. He trembles all over, and then his release jets violently into the air, spattering my face and the front of my tunic. The ragged sound he makes as he comes is almost a groan, but he doesn't move. He just quakes, as if holding himself locked into place is taking every bit of energy he has, and his seed covers my hands and face as it spurts out of him. He seems to come forever, so I squeeze him with my hand and run my fingers along his sac, telling him how much he turns me on and how good he feels in my grip.

When Victor's finally done, he lets out the most contented sigh I've ever heard, his eyes closing. He licks his lips, the tip of his tongue grazing the side of one tusk, and it makes my pussy clench at the sight of it. "Did...I hurt you?"

"Not at all." I lift my hand carefully from his now-sticky cock, and sure enough, I'm fine. "The question is, did I hurt *you*?"

"Never. That was...better than anything." He sounds dazed. Utterly dazed. "Bee. I've never..."

"It's okay," I promise him, sliding between his thighs again and pressing against his chest. He's sticky with his release, but I'm covered in it, too, so hey. I kiss him, tender affection for this big, brutish alien rushing through me. "You don't have to explain anything at all, Victor. I know."

He groans and kisses me, cupping my face in his hands as if I'm the most precious thing he's ever seen. His lips brush mine, and then he pulls his hand away, frowning at the wetness there. "Did I spray your face?"

"You sprayed everything," I say with a giggle. "I'm afraid you're going to have to shower again."

His mouth curves into a slow grin. "It was worth it. I'll shower six times a day if you'll put your hands on me. That's my new prize," he says. "Your touch. Every day. Every night."

"We'll see." But parts of me are already clenching at the thought. "Let's go shower and then we'll make dinner."

I slip out of his grip and he gets to his feet, stretching languidly. He must feel good, I think with pride. I *made* him feel that good.

As he pads toward the bathroom, I notice blood streaking his skin. I gasp, horrified. "Victor! Your back!" He reaches out to touch one shoulder, and it takes me a moment to realize his spikes are gone.

They've receded into his skin.

19

VICTOR

*H*ours later, I lie awake in bed. Bee is in my arms, her small body cupped by my larger one. I hold her tightly, loving that I can do this finally. I do not want this moment to end. Ever. I bury my nose in her fragrant mane and breathe deep, utterly content.

Had I known this sort of joy would be waiting for me, I would never have raised a finger against any of the guardsmen. Being with Bee is more satisfying than tearing out a thousand throats or outwitting a thousand guards. Nowhere in my memories stolen from Crulden the Ruiner is there such... contentment. But here with Bee, listening to her sleep, taking in her scent, I am at peace.

My spikes have receded into my flesh once more. The moment they did, I realized it was because I finally feel relaxed enough to not be on guard constantly. I don't need to protect myself from Bee. Here, at her side, I'm free to enjoy life, and so there's no need to protect myself from unseen enemies. They'll spring forth again if I'm threatened—or if Bee is—but for now, I'm able to curl around my mate and sleep in the same narrow bed with her.

My mate. I taste the word on my tongue and I like it. Bee doesn't know it yet, but she's my mate. She proved to me tonight that just because my body is fearsome, we can still share pleasure. Perhaps someday the barbs on my cock will recede as well, though I do not have memories of that. It doesn't matter. I enjoyed Bee's hands and her words. I enjoyed her mouth on mine. If that is all I can have, I will be more than content with it. Touching me pleased her, too. Her arousal scent drifted through the air all night long, as she showed me how to work the machines in the kitchen to make dinner and then to clean up. I thought my hands would feel naked and useless without my claws, but I can touch the buttons on the machines with ease.

More than that, I can touch Bee without fear of drawing blood.

We kissed a few more times before bed, but Bee did not let things go further than a kiss. When I asked about pleasuring her, she said she wanted this night to be about me and not her. Then she kissed me again, sweetly enough to distract me.

But hours have passed, and I am still awake. If I am reading the comm panel in the bedroom correctly (as she has shown me), the time has now rolled over into the next day.

Which means I am free to make this day about her pleasure, instead of mine.

I run a hand down Bee's side. She is all curves and softness, this female, so small against my larger form. At my touch, she stirs in her sleep, sighing before pressing back against me. All curves and softness...and a heavy sleeper. Amused, I brush my lips over the top of her head. I want to kiss her neck, but at this angle, it's simply not possible. So I will just have to do other things to pleasure her. I run my fingers lightly down her side again, and when she instinctively rolls toward me, I cup one heavy teat in my hand. Such large, fascinating globes, with such sensitive tips. I think about how she scraped them against my chest, teasing herself as she kissed me. I drag my thumb over the tip, teasing it until it hardens under my touch.

She moans, rubbing her backside against me. "Victor..."

Did she just call for me in her sleep? I pause, and when she doesn't move or protest, my heart swells with pride. My female. She wants me even when she sleeps. She dreams of me. *Me.* Not that handsome mesakkah idiot she claimed to "date."

"Mine," I whisper, toying with her nipple through the fabric of her tunic. She whimpers and presses against my hand, craving more, and her arousal scent floods the air around me. "My Bee."

She rolls onto her back, and that gives me access to her other full teat. Fascinated, I tug on her tunic, pulling it up and revealing warm skin. "Mmm...Victor?" Her eyes open a slit and she looks at me with dazed confusion. "Are you okay? Can you not sleep?"

Her hand goes to my mane, and she smooths it back from my face affectionately, her fingers drifting over one of my tufted ears. I press my mouth to the soft belly I've exposed and brush my lips over her skin. "I want to touch you, Bee. I want to do for you like you did for me. I want to give you pleasure."

A little moan escapes her, and fresh arousal soaks the air around us. "Oh," she breathes. "Victor, you...don't have to. I like touching you. It wasn't tit for tat." Her fingers toy in my hair. "Wanted to make you feel good."

"I want to touch you," I repeat again. "Your scent is making me mad with need, Bee." I lap at her navel with my tongue, wanting to lick her all over. "Let me caress you. Let me rub your cunt and slake your need. Please."

Bee whimpers again, but she tugs her tunic up above her teats, revealing them to my gaze. It's a silent invitation for more, and I fall upon her hungrily, thrilled that I get this chance to give my mate the pleasure she deserves. Now that her skin is exposed, I can see that those fascinating nipples are a deeper shade than the rest of her skin, tight and pointing up at my mouth as if in a silent demand to be tasted. I flick my tongue over one, and Bee gasps, her thighs coming apart in another silent request.

Kef me, this female is going to destroy me. I'm never leaving this bed again, not as long as she's in it. With a hungry growl, I nip at the taut tip of one breast, then my greedy mouth moves to the other to give it attention. I lick one, then the other, and when she wriggles with pleasure, panting, she digs her fingers into my mane, holding me to her teats. The heavy globes slide against her sides, so I cup each one as I taste it, feeding it to my hungry mouth. I want to feast on these gorgeous teats forever, play with them endlessly, because she's making such sweet, needy sounds as I do, and all the while, her arousal scent grows thicker and thicker around us.

I think about how she'd touched me, and how she squeezed my shaft and dragged her fingers through the wetness on the tip of my cock. I want to do the same to her—to give her touches between her legs that make her wild with pleasure. I lift my mouth from one glorious teat to glance up at her. "Can I touch your cunt, Bee?"

She moans, nodding as she clutches at my head. Her thighs spread apart, and the scent of her nearly overwhelms me with need. I latch onto one of her nipples again, teasing and sucking, and press my hand between her thighs, exploring her. She did not wear trou to bed, wishing to be comfortable, and I am grateful for it. There's a scrap of material covering her cunt, and when I discover it with searching fingers, I growl in frustration and push it aside, because I *need* her cunt exposed to me.

"Victor," she pants. "Oh, Victor."

My searching fingers uncover a crinkle of curls over the

mound of her cunt. I find these fascinating, but not nearly as fascinating as the slippery wet folds underneath those curls. She is soaked, my pretty Bee, my fingertips gliding through her folds with such ease that it makes my cock ache. So wet for me. I drag my fingers through those soft petals of flesh, grateful again that my claws are gone. Now I have the freedom to touch and explore her as I like, and I trace her folds with one fingertip, then the seam between them, then deeper still. I find the entrance to her body, the one that leads inside her, and dip into it with a fingertip. That elicits a moan from her, but her most fascinating reaction comes when I brush over the bead of flesh at the apex of her cunt. It is rounded and prominent, and when I rub my fingertip against it, her legs jerk and she makes a garbled sound, her fingers tightening in my mane.

Perhaps this is the most sensitive spot, then. I lick the nipple I'm teasing and lift my head to ask, when the thick, heady scent of her overwhelms me. Bee's juicy cunt is coating my hand with her delicious scent, and I *need* to taste it. I lift my hand to my mouth and lick my fingers.

Oh.

Oh *kef.*

I let out a long, ragged groan. "Oh, Bee. That cunt is *juicy*. I've never tasted anything better."

She whimpers, squirming on the blankets. "Victor," she pants. "Touch me."

"Can I use my tongue? I *need* to use my tongue," I clarify. "I need to taste all of you."

"Please," she says again. "Please, please. I need you so much."

I love how wild she is. How frantic. She's as hungry for my mouth as I am for her touch. Smugly, I think how the other male never elicited any response from her. A mere touch from me and Bee's cunt soaks with honey. In this, I am a champion, and I am eager to use my champion skills to make my mate come harder than she ever has before.

With wild, eager presses of my mouth to her belly, I ease down her rounded body and then between her thighs. Her clothing is still in the way, so I guide her legs together and pull it down her limbs, tossing it aside like rubbish. It's in my way. I want her cunt exposed to the air, exposed to my tongue. And now that she's naked, I feast on the sight of her.

Bee's cunt is just as lovely to gaze upon as it is to touch. Her folds are duskier than the rest of her golden-brown skin, drawing the eye in silent invitation. She's so wet that her skin gleams, the curls above her slit damp. I run a teasing finger up and down, spreading her softness for my gaze, and she moans, her abundant thighs going wide again. Gleaming amidst those folds is the sensitive pearl of flesh that's makes her react, and I can't wait to get my mouth on it.

I suck my fingers clean of her taste as I use my other hand to rub her cunt. She squirms against my touch, panting, and it makes her teats jiggle enticingly. "Unfair," I murmur, licking the last of her juices from my skin. "I want my mouth all over you, but I can only put it one place at a time." When she makes another needy sound, I chuckle, feeling strong and powerful to make such a beautiful female so hungry for my touch. "Lucky for you, I know where I want it most."

"Don't make me beg," she warns.

"You're already begging," I remind her, and slide to the end of the bed. It's such a small, ridiculous bed clearly made for humans and not anyone larger. It's almost a relief to kneel on the floor and just haul her down toward where I'm waiting to taste her. I tug one thigh over my shoulder, grateful again that my spikes have receded, because it allows me to do this. I hook her other leg as well and then nuzzle my face against her cunt, drowning in the scent of her.

She cries out, the sound sweet to my ears.

As for me, I am lost. I have been dreaming of the taste of her for weeks now, and this is sensory overload. Like the ravenous beast I am, I bury my face in her folds and tongue her. My world ceases to exist outside of the cradle of her wet cunt, and I lick every bit of delicious wetness from her body, needing more and more with every stroke of my tongue. Bee's hands twist in my mane and she cries out as I lap at her, but she does not come. It takes me a moment to realize that I have been selfishly seeking my own pleasure, not hers. She needs that sensitive little bead teased, and I have been sating myself on her juices. With a determined growl, I move up to the little bud and trace the tip of my tongue around it.

Bee sucks in a breath, her hips arching. Her hands tremble against my scalp. "Victor!"

"I am here," I tell her, and then lick that bead again. "Is this what you like?"

She makes a low keening noise in her throat, her thighs tightening around my neck. "Oh please, Victor. Please, please, please. Make me come. I need it."

I want to tell her that I have her. That I will not let her go until I make her come better than she has ever come before. That she is my mate and I am claiming her with every stroke of my tongue on this gorgeous cunt. But all of that would require lifting my mouth, and I am greedy enough to keep tonguing her, making sure to drag the flat of my tongue against the nub with every pass.

"My clit," she tells me, panting. "Tease the hood of my clit just like that."

A clit? Is that what it is called? I make a mental note of this and do as she asks, and I love that she is bold enough to demand this from me. "Tell me how you like it," I murmur between licks. "So I can give you the best orgasm."

And she does. She tells me to speed up, to keep my movements steady, where I should rub my tongue against her clit (the underside) and when to add a finger into the tight well of warmth that is her channel. The act of adding a finger nearly makes me come unglued—her body squeezes it tightly. I imagine what it would feel like for her to accept my cock like this—to take me into her cunt and grip down on it like a vise, and I thrust into the air pointlessly even as I pleasure her. A low trembling starts in her body, and I add a second finger, feeling her stretch around me, and hot need dribbles down my length. I am hard and aching once more, but I keep my mouth on her, teasing her clit and sucking on it as she instructs, and when she comes, it is with a hard cry and a fresh burst of her flavor that nearly sends me over myself.

I lick her clean, reveling in the taste of her as her cunt squeezes and flutters around my pumping fingers, and when she finally sighs with satisfaction, I feel as if I have won a dozen tournaments. Nothing in my stolen memories compares to the dewy sheen on Bee's golden skin, or the taste of her permanently etched into my hide. Nothing is better than the little noise of protest she makes when my fingers slide free from her cunt, as if she misses my body.

It will be enough.

"God almighty," Bee says hoarsely, pressing the back of one hand to her brow as I pepper kisses along the insides of her thighs and scrape my tusks against her skin. She's so soft and perfect that I want to keep touching her, always. "You're good with that mouth of yours."

"I am a champion," I agree. "Can I...make you come again?"

She sits up on her elbows, staring at me. "So soon?" When I nod, her thighs primly clasp together. "I need time to come down, Victor. You..." A look of understanding crosses her face and she pats the bed next to her. "You need to come, don't you?"

"Again. Yes. Touching you felt so good. I wanted it to be just about you, but...parts of me do not listen well."

Bee chuckles and scoots over to the edge of the narrow bed. When I get to my feet, her eyes widen at my cock, painfully erect and leaking. "Oh, yeah, I can take care of that for you." Her voice turns to a throaty purr. "Come lie next to me. I'll make you feel good."

In this moment, I do not care that I am too big for the bed. I do as she commands, not caring that my feet (and most of my calves) dangle over the edge, or that my big torso swallows the bed like this, stealing all the room from her. I do not care because she tugs her tunic off, exposing her glorious body to me. She leans over, her teats brushing against my thigh as one hand goes to toy with my sac and her mouth closes over the tip of my cock.

In this moment, I do not care about anything at all but Bee. Bee and her sucking mouth, Bee and her teasing fingers, Bee and her incredible scent.

I am completely and utterly hers.

20

Three Weeks Later

BEE

I'm humming as I do the dishes. Since Victor made breakfast, the cleaning falls to me. It's hard not to be happy when your man loves to cook and he woke you up with a pussy-licking that still makes my knees tremble an hour later. I smile to myself at that thought. My man. He's not really my man, but it's fun to imagine. There's nothing official between us. It's mutual pleasuring, me using my body to encourage Victor into model behavior. There's been no talk of the future, and I've learned not to look too far ahead.

I'm enjoying the moment too much.

I peek outside and bite back a laugh at the sight that greets me. For a week now, Victor has been talking about how "untidy" the rock path looks. How the stones don't follow any sort of order and how the colors are all over the place. He's out there organizing them right now, hauling the rocks out of the ground and sorting them into piles by color and size. I have no doubt that when he's done, the path will look fantastic.

I've learned a few things about Victor in the last few weeks. He loves being outdoors. That isn't surprising to me—for an alien who spent his first several weeks in a cage and then constantly trapped in one room, of course he does. He wanted to start a garden, but because of my allergies, he's not able to dig up the soil. It was incredibly disappointing for him, though he said he understood, so I talked with Akris, and a week later, we acquired several small fruit tree saplings. They're not native to the planet and will need constant care, but Victor was thrilled with them. I've never seen a man filled with such joy. He hugged me a dozen times (and then licked me senseless that night). He even thanked the guards. I've never seen Herrix speechless. Now every day, Victor tends to his trees, and he's so damn proud of his tiny orchard that it makes me ache.

Victor is also a neat freak. The pump house is gleamingly clean, all the rust gone from the controls. The yard is tidy and we keep the house in perfect shape. It took about a week or so for Victor to come around to the idea that the house was much more enjoyable when it was clean, and now he's constantly tidying up. I think he likes having control over his environment. Of course, he always tells me that it's just because he wants to be the best, and that includes at tidying.

Our days have settled into a quiet routine. Maybe it's boring to a gladiator who is used to a life of excitement, but Victor seems happy. We eat our meals together, we clean together, we sleep together, and Victor tends his trees while I go through my messages. We have lessons on everything, from the air-sled that we borrow from Herrix and Akris to drive around the property, to simple math and learning how to read. Victor devours any and all information with single-minded intent...and then demands a reward later that night.

And oh god, the rewards system is killing me in all the best ways.

Victor demands rewards day and night, and because I'm as addicted to him as he is to me, I happily give them up. We've touched each other in every way possible under the sun, except for when it comes to his cock. He refuses to even consider having sex with me, so we kiss and rub and lick our way to pleasure multiple times a day. I wake up to having my pussy eaten out more often than not, and when I don't, I pout over breakfast until Victor tosses me onto the table and feasts on me. Maybe this wild need for each other will slow down over time, but for now, I'm dizzy with the intensity of our relationship and loving every moment of it.

The comm panel chirps, an indication that someone's waiting to connect. I bite back a groan, wiping my wet hands, and then peek out at Victor. He's still in the front yard, moving paving stones, and my nose twitches as the earth is turned over. He's very careful about it, because he doesn't like it when I suffer. I don't want to point out that even this small movement is playing havoc with my senses, because I know he likes to work outside in the sunlight. I rub the side of my nose as the panel chirps again, and then head over to answer it.

First Rank Novis's stern blue face fills the screen. "Female," he greets. "You look well enough."

I smile sweetly, gritting my teeth. I've corrected Novis on the whole "female" thing enough times at this point that I know he's doing that nonsense on purpose, so I'm determined to ignore it. "This is a pleasure, First Rank. How are you doing today? Enjoying this lovely weather?"

"It is sufficient." He pulls up a data pad and studies it. "I would like an update on the subject. Has he shown any signs of aggression in the last week? Any anger issues?" He looks up from his pad. "Have his eyes turned red?"

It's like he doesn't listen to a single word I say. "Of course not." I keep smiling, hoping it'll make my tone less saccharine when I really want to just scream in frustration. "Victor has been a model student." I use that instead of the word "subject" because it irritates me when people don't see Victor as a person, just a project. "Zero signs of aggression. Zero instances of his eyes turning red. I told you that his spikes have receded, right? We determined that it was because he no longer feels on edge, as if he has to protect himself. He's learning to trust, First Rank, and he's flourishing in a stable environment."

"Mmm." He moves his fingers over the pad, writing something down. "How are his lessons going?"

"Very well," I say brightly, pleased I can at last extoll Victor's virtues to the people in charge. "He's incredibly smart. Every lesson we have is so he can function in society here, but he's already moved past the rudimentary basics, so we're focusing on math skills and some reading this week."

"Reading?" That makes Novis look up. "What's he reading?"

"Right now, I'm just teaching him the basics of human English," I begin. "He—"

"Human English? Why would he need to learn that?" His lip curls dismissively. "If you're going to teach him, it should be Homeworld Basic, not a useless language from the far end of the galaxy."

"Oh, goodness, it's not useless at all," I simper, mentally envisioning wrapping my hands around Novis's throat and shaking him. "Why, he needs to learn how to fit in with the people here on Risda III, and all of the people here are, for the most part, human." I widen my smile. "As for Homeworld Basic, I'm more than happy to teach him that, but someone has to teach me first." I wink at Novis, as if we're sharing a secret. "I'd be surprised if any human has picked it up. It's so complex, though your faith in me to teach such a thing is so very thoughtful."

Novis grunts. "I guess if he shows aptitude with the human scribblings, that'll be good enough for now."

"Exactly," I coo. "Unless you had plans for him to leave Risda III, I think communicating with the women here is his best bet."

"Is he exercising? Working on keeping muscle mass?"

That feels like a loaded question, so I twist it a little. "Victor loves gardening, actually! You should see how well he takes care of the little trees that Akris got for him."

"Akris?" He tilts his head in that way that mesakkah do, indicating they're surprised.

"Yes! They've become good friends, Victor, Akris, and Herrix. We have them over for dinner some nights." I keep smiling, because I do like that the men have formed a friendship, even if it's slightly competitive and involves footraces or who can throw a rock to hit a mark a hundred paces away. "I think it's good for Victor to be comfortable around other people as well as me. You can ask the men their opinions of him—I'm quite sure they'll match mine. He truly is excelling in all areas." And because it makes me giggle inwardly, I add, "A champion of a student."

First Rank Novis taps a few more things into his pad. "I see. Thank you for your report. No incidents to note?"

"None at all."

He nods, and that's my cue that the comm is cutting off. Novis isn't much of one for chatter, and really, that suits me just fine. The moment the vid panel goes dark, I breathe a sigh of relief, rubbing my neck. For some reason, the weekly check-ins always make me tense up. I feel as if they're trying to catch me in a lie, and part of it is just my desperate need to make things as perfect as possible for Victor so they know how amazing he is.

More than that, they can't know that we're sleeping together, or that Victor's straw-filled mattress in the tiny side room goes unused. That we shower together and that Victor greets me in the morning by giving me head. If our relationship comes out, my credibility will be ruined. They won't believe me when I say that Victor isn't violent, or that he's intelligent and restrained enough to be treated like a regular person. They'll think I'm dickmatized and I'll be removed from my position, Victor will be back in a cage, and all of the hard work he's done will be negated.

I won't let that happen.

It's meant jumping through a few hoops for the last month, of course. I didn't lie when I said that Herrix and Akris come over for dinner. I also didn't point out that I scrub every inch of my skin twice before they come over so they don't smell my arousal, and that we claim our scents are mingled because I throw our laundry in the washer together. They think we're good friends and that I'm a generous, probably somewhat idiotic human female for working with Victor.

No one can know that his smile makes me light up with pure joy. That the feel of his tusks on the inside of my knee makes my pussy clench reflexively, or that I can't sleep unless he's curled around me in our small bed at night. That we link fingers and go to sleep talking about trees, or the weather, or the future here on Risda.

I don't know how long it all has to be secret. I just know that right now, it absolutely does.

There's a light rap at the front door, and Victor pokes his head in, wiping dirt from his fingers. The tickle in my nose returns, and I rub it, fighting back a sneeze. "What did Novis want?" Victor asks.

"You know," I tell him tartly. "You heard everything."

He grins at me, looking like a wicked little boy. "Figured that out, did you?"

I'd suspected it after he let a few things drop in conversation throughout the week, things that I hadn't told him but had mentioned on the vid-calls with Novis. His naughty smile confirms it, though. "You're the nosiest man," I chide, though I'm not really upset. I'd want to know what people were saying about me, too. "I gave you a glowing report. I said that you were smart, and strong, and that you have the best tongue I've ever sat on."

Victor throws his head back and laughs, the sound pure delight. It makes my belly flutter with pleasure, and I hope he's always that happy.

If I have anything to say about it, he will.

"Liked sitting on my tongue, did you?" He stalks inside with a predator's grace, a gleam in his eyes that makes my pulse speed up.

"You know I did," I tell him, breathless. I still haven't recovered from straddling his cheeks last night as he fucked me with his tongue.

"Good," Victor purrs. "It's time for my reward, anyhow."

"It's barely past breakfast," I protest, my voice as weak as my knees. "You...maybe we should..."

He looms over me, all sexy, confident alien, and the twitching in my nose from the soil is not nearly as noticeable as the twitching in my body at his nearness. "You should sit on my face and I should tongue you until you scream my name again? Why, I'd be delighted, Bee."

"I...you..."

"I'm going to wash my hands," he murmurs, leaning in so close that I can feel his hot breath fanning my hair. "And then I'm going to kef that sweet cunt with my tongue until you soak my mane. Because I deserve it."

God, how can I possibly argue with that?

Two days later, we're woken at dawn by the comm panel's annoying chirp.

I groan, trying to burrow deeper into the bed. "Novis is an asshole to call this early." Victor's big, heavy arm is tossed over my shoulders, and I clutch it against my breasts, because he's warm and delicious. "Ignore it. Maybe it'll go away."

He massages my breasts, teasing my nipples. "I am awake now."

A whine escapes me, because parts of me are now waking up, too. "Unfair," I pant. "I wanted to sleep longer."

"You sleep. I'll work." His hand leaves my breasts and hitches up my sleep tunic, baring my ass. "I'm finding myself rather hungry." Victor caresses my buttocks, then slips his fingers between my thighs from behind, stroking my pussy.

Well, I'm awake now, too. I rock against his seeking hand, gasping when he thrusts one large finger deep inside me. I twist my fingers against the blankets, looking for something to hold onto as he tugs my hips up—

The comm chirps again. And again.

Victor growls, his hand sliding away. His fingers leave my body with a wet sound. "I'll get it."

I bite back my frustration as he gets to his feet, licking his hand. I guess my orgasm has to wait a few minutes. "Answer in the living area," I tell him, running a hand through my dark curls. He's going to want to talk to me, too, so I'd better get dressed. "Tell him he needs a hobby."

Chuckling, Victor slips out of the bedroom, buck naked, and I suspect he intends on giving Novis an eyeful out of revenge. While that makes me smile, it also reminds me that I need to dress quickly, because we can't look as if we rolled out of bed together. I grab my clothes and shove my legs through my pants, swapping out my wrinkled sleep tunic for a fresh one. By the time I drag my hair up into a knot and head out into the living area, I look reasonable.

When I go into the living room, though, Victor has his back to me, his tail twitching over his taut buttocks. I can tell from the set of his shoulders that he's on edge, and there's a series of hard points appearing under the skin of his back, which tells me his spikes are going to pop soon.

"Good morning," I say brightly, and then feign surprise. "Oh, Victor, you're not dressed. Did I interrupt something?"

He moves to the side, glancing at me, and I finally notice the face on the comm screen. It's not Novis at all. It's Lord va'Rin.

I bite back a gasp of shock, because this is completely unexpected. It's always First Rank Novis that checks in on us. Whenever I ask about Lord va'Rin lately, I'm told he's busy, or he's off-planet, or he's in meetings. The impression I get is that he has no time for Victor, so it's startling to see him right now. "Lovely to see you, my lord," I say, putting on my brightest smile. I try not to look over at Victor, because if I do, I'm going to cringe at his blatant nudity. "It's nice of you to check in on Victor's progress."

Lord va'Rin gives us both a studied look. I keep smiling, even though I feel like a faker under his stern gaze. Lord va'Rin probably isn't much older than Victor or myself, but he always looks so proper and somber that I feel like a child in front of him. A naughty, naughty child, I add mentally, thinking of Victor and how he licked his fingers before he came in here.

The lord tilts his head, his long, smooth black hair gleaming almost as brightly as his polished, metallic horns. "Do you often greet your callers in such a fashion, Victor?"

"Only when they call at dawn," Victor retorts, crossing his arms.

Lord va'Rin immediately asks, "Am I interrupting something?"

"Of course not," I chime in, beaming. "We're happy to see you at any hour."

A ghost of a smile curves Lord va'Rin's mouth. "It is indeed early. You'll have to forgive me. I've just returned from being off-world and my schedule is awry." His focus turns to Victor. "I've heard interesting things about your progress. Both First Rank Novis and several of his guardsmen speak highly of your transformation. They say that under Bee's tutelage, you have shown yourself to be non-violent and capable, adaptable, and most of all, willing. In fact, the reports I have received are downright glowing."

I clasp my hands in front of my chin, utterly delighted at the praise Victor's receiving. I want to blurt out his praises, but this moment is for him, not for me. I want him to feel good with all he's accomplished.

Victor only grunts. "I'm not a monster."

"I know you are not. In fact, one of the other clones of Crulden the Ruiner is settled quite happily here on Risda III. That's how I knew you had the potential of being something different than what you were created for. He set a good example. And after glowing reports from"—he glances down, checking something off screen—"Guardsmen Herrix, Akris, Riffin, and First Rank Novis, all of whom have thoroughly interacted with you, I'd like to offer you a position."

I go still the moment Riffin's name is brought up. My mind immediately races—what is he thinking? What new angle is Riffin pursuing? I thought he realized we were done. It's too much for me to hope that he'd come to understand that we're not meant to be together and decided to be the bigger man. Even aliens can be petty. I'm so focused on what Riffin might be up to that it takes a moment for the rest to sink in.

"Position?" Victor asks, a frown on his face.

"Yes. You've proven that you can be trusted, and I've been told that you've got the pump house working in top shape." That small smile plays on Lord va'Rin's mouth again. "So I'd like to offer you a position at another pump house farther down the coast. There's a cottage on the shore I've put aside for you. It's a bit more of a remote location, but it has an excellent garden and orchard, and you'll be well-paid and given an air-sled of your own."

Victor is silent for a long moment. He rubs his chin and then glances over at me. "I...do like a garden. But what about Bee?"

This time, Lord va'Rin's smile is wider. "Bee has shown me that the humans do indeed need a social worker to champion them. You'll have your position, and I've let the port manager know that you're to have an office in town, centrally located, as well as a house of your choosing. We can work out the details of your pay."

Oh.

Oh. This is wonderful. At least, it should be wonderful. I can't help but feel there's something I'm missing. "Thank you, Lord va'Rin." When he nods, I glance over at Victor, grinning. "You can help me set up my office with that air-sled of yours."

"Actually..." Lord va'Rin's mouth flattens. "Victor will not be close. The position I am offering is on the coast. I have a guard-station there and Victor would be near them. It's quite a lovely stretch of land, but I'm afraid it's nowhere near the human settlements."

Oh. "I see."

Victor takes one look at my face and storms out. I fight back my disappointment, managing a smile somehow. "That wasn't a temper tantrum, by the way. I think he's just a little over-whelmed—"

Lord va'Rin chuckles. "You do not have to defend him to me. I know the difference between frustration and a rampage. I've actually spent quite a bit of time with Crulden's other clone, who goes by the name of Mycrul. They're very similar in some ways and completely different in others. As long as there are no red eyes and spikes, I'm not concerned. But now that we may speak privately, I wanted to ask you..." He gives me a searching look. "You seem unhappy with my offer for employment. Is it not what you wanted?"

Am I that obvious? I always work so hard to disguise my true feelings. It's just... "You're sending Victor away."

The lord nods. "I am. Make no mistake, I think you have worked wonders with him, and I have every confidence in Victor himself. I feel he is trustworthy, and so I want him to have a job where he has the freedom to do as he likes. I want him to be happy."

I swallow hard and manage a bright nod. "I understand."

"You don't," he says, just as kindly. "You think perhaps he should have stayed in Port? What job in Port do you think he would be content with? Consider not only Victor's needs, but that of Port's residents. Where would you place him?"

With me, I want to say, but I know what Lord va'Rin is getting at. Would the people of Port view Victor as a terrifying problem, or would they accept him? I know his face is fearsome, his form terrifying. I know he started out in a constant state of fury and a few months is not enough time to determine if he can be completely safe around the others on his own. I know that the women in Port are largely scared of aliens and have abusive pasts.

I have no idea what would be best for him. I just know that I'm in love with him, and if word of that gets out, it might ruin this new job for him, a job with a garden, and trees, and the freedom to do as he pleases.

So I simply smile and thank Lord va'Rin for the job offers. "It's very thoughtful of you. I'm sure Victor will love the shore."

21

VICTOR

*B*ee is sending me away.

I listen to her conversation with the mesakkah lord, and I hate every word of it. She doesn't disagree with him when he says my new position will be far away from town. That I can't intermingle with the residents of Port just yet. That I'll be far enough away from her that we won't be able to see each other. Instead of saying that it isn't what she wants, that she wants to keep me, Bee laughs and smiles and discusses the office she will have in town. She is eager to help the women of Port, she confesses to him when they end the comm.

And then she sighs softly to herself.

She does not cry. She does not weep that I am going to be leaving her. Bee is silent in the other room, and I clench my fists, wishing my claws were back, because then I would be able to dig them into my skin. I could rip at the walls here in this small cottage and show my fierce anger and frustration and rage.

But Bee likes these painted walls. They make her happy. And Bee makes me happy.

So I go outside and return to working on the stone path. I have been making it better, just because I like for things to be the best. There is no point to working on it, not now when we are about to leave this place, but I need to do something with my hands.

Bee did not ask me to stay. She is ready for me to go.

And I...I will never be ready to leave her side. But if she does not want to keep me, I will not force myself upon her. I need Bee's smiles and companionship more than anything else in this world, more than her kisses on my cock or her gentle, squeezing hands. I need her laughter and her voice and her very personality. I need *Bee.*

I want to rip the stone path up and fling the rocks over the cliff, but seeing disappointment in Bee's eyes would hurt more than anything. So I stew on my frustration and sadness, and wonder what it will be like to have trees and a garden, but no Bee.

THINGS ARE strange between us after the discussion with Lord va'Rin. Bee busies herself with packing up the small house, chatting animatedly to me about how nice it'll be for me to have a garden without her sneezes, and the fresh vegetables I can grow. That we can re-pot my small saplings and have them transported to the new house. That I'll make new friends with the guards at the other outpost, and that it'll be nice for me to live by the shore. That the coast is lovely and temperate and she thinks I'll adore it.

Bee talks and talks, her words and smiles trying to convince me that I should love the job waiting for me.

I am silent, because I cannot agree. Perhaps a garden will be nice, but I would rather have Bee. Perhaps the shore will be nice, but I would rather have Bee. Perhaps the new job will be interesting...

But I would rather have Bee.

Everything comes back to Bee. I would clean floors and shovel mud if it meant I got to spend the rest of my days with Bee at my side.

She says nothing about our parting, though. She smiles and talks and smiles and talks. Bee does not say she will miss me. She says she is happy for me. Excited.

I am miserable. Completely and utterly miserable.

I never thought beyond being with Bee in this moment, in this house. I did not think about a future, or that we would not have one together. It feels so natural to be with her, as if we have always been together, have always been laughing together, breathing in each other's scents. It is special to me.

But it is also becoming clear that it is not special to Bee, and perhaps that is what hurts the most.

THAT NIGHT, Bee sets up my bed in the other room. "In case one of the others comes by early, we should make sure they don't think there's anything going on between us," she says softly. "I don't want to jeopardize anything for you."

I grunt a response.

If my lack of commentary hurts Bee's feelings, she hides it well. She fusses over my bed, squeezes my hand goodnight, and then retreats into her room and shuts the door behind her. I wait, listening. As I have learned with the others that called me "Asshole" for the first few weeks, people say many things behind doors that they will not say to your face. Most do not realize I have excellent hearing, and so I hear a lot of things I am not meant to.

All is silent in Bee's room, however.

She is not sad I am leaving. Maybe all this time, all she has valued is her job.

It seems wrong, but I cannot shake the feeling of it.

THE NEXT DAY, Herrix and Akris arrive and put the trunk into the back of the air-sled. I am fully dressed, my mane combed out, the high collar of a new tunic tugging at my neck, and new shoes pinching my wide feet. I hate all of it, even if Herrix and Akris tease me like friends over just how miserable I look.

"I think he looks very nice," Bee chides them in her sweet way. "Very professional."

I do not want to be professional. I want to be *hers*.

I tug at the collar, wishing that it were less choking or that I didn't have to wear a tunic at all. Bee has spoiled me at our small cottage, letting me wander about in nothing but trou. I feel ridiculous in this get-up, but her smile is brilliant as she gazes up at me. "Handsome," she declares. "So very handsome."

But not enough to keep, it seems.

We head in to Port, the air-sled coasting through the sky. It's a lovely day, the weather mild and full of sunshine. Bee clasps my hand as we sit in the back seat, giving it an encouraging squeeze. She says nothing, her expression distracted as Akris and Herrix chat about how many females are now in Port. Herrix has his eye on one in particular, but Akris isn't interested in a human female. He says his mother will hang him by his tail if he mates with anyone other than a good mesakkah female. Herrix just rolls his eyes at that, and the banter continues. Normally I'd find it fascinating to listen in on their thoughts, but today, I just want to talk to Bee. I want to turn this sled around and go back to our colorful cottage. I want to bury my face between her thighs and forget that Lord va'Rin ever contacted us.

The air-sled lands just outside of Port, though, and with it, my spirits plummet. "This is where we split up," Herrix announces cheerfully. "I'm taking this sled back to Lord va'Rin's. Akris will show you to your new office, Bee. Victor, you're with me. We're stopping by the port medic's office and then you're off to your new posting."

"So soon?" A look of panic crosses Bee's face and she clutches at my arm. "Oh, but..."

Herrix glances over at me. My misery must be obvious. He falters momentarily, watching me and then reluctantly tearing his gaze away. "Uh, actually, I have some errands to run. I can come back and get Victor later? At the end of the day?"

"That'd be lovely," Bee says in her too-bright, too-charming voice. "Victor can help me set up my office."

Akris nods. "That'd work. You need to go to the medic first, though. Lord va'Rin's orders."

I shrug. It doesn't matter. Not much does. I no longer feel like a champion—Bee's champion. I feel rejected. Unwanted. Above all, melancholy and heartsick. *My mate*, I say silently. Even if she does not want me, Bee is my mate. Now and forever.

NEITHER MYSELF NOR Bee are very talkative as Akris escorts us across town. He brings me to the Port medic's office, then heads off with Bee, promising to return soon enough as I'm sent through a barrage of medical tests and my blood is taken. Once upon a time, I might have fought the tired-looking mesakkah male that pricks my finger and makes records in his data pad, but after being with Bee, I know he's just doing his job. He's not trying to anger me.

"You're extremely healthy," the medic says.

I snort. "Of course I am. I am bred to be a champion."

The medic smiles. "Truth. Well, I have the information Lord va'Rin requested. Did you have anything specifically that you wanted done?"

That makes me pause, because I don't understand what he's asking. "Want done?" I echo. "What do you mean?"

He gestures at his data-pad. "Lord va'Rin is offering to pay for any sort of cosmetic procedures you wish to have done. It's not easy having the same face as a notorious gladiator, so if you want to change anything, I'm letting you know that it's taken care of. Removing claws and tusks, of course. Not adding anything for battle." The medic frowns to himself at the thought. "Perhaps I should have specified."

Have my tusks and claws removed? My claws are already filed down. And I like my tusks because Bee likes my tusks. Do they make my mouth a little odd? Sure. But I love the sound she makes when I drag them over the inside of one soft thigh. "I like looking fearsome," I say, thinking of Bee. "In case...someone... needs protecting."

"Mate?" The medic pauses, smiling.

I shrug. It seems foolish to assume that someone with my face would ever get a mate.

He grunts at my silence. "Thought I'd ask. The other Crulden clone did."

That gets my attention. "He what?"

"Had his tusks removed. Wanted to kiss his female properly."

"His...female?"

The medic nods, flicking through his data pad without looking up at me. "Yes. Tiny little scrap of a human. Small body, big attitude. He seems quite happy with her though."

The other clone of Crulden has a mate? And this is accepted? No one is afraid for the female? I lean in. "Did he... does he have barbs on his cock?"

"Nope. You do?" At my expression, he nods, continuing. "That's the praxiian part of the genetics for you. We can have those removed if you like. Most praxiians have them removed at birth. It's a simple enough procedure. Your skin would be sensitive for a few days afterwards, but it's easy enough to do."

I can have the barbs on my cock removed...now that Bee is abandoning me. The irony of the situation is not lost. "I am surprised the other Crulden has a mate."

"He's quite taken with her. They've been together for months now, or so I've been told." The medic smiles. "Lord va'Rin went off-world to go buy her for Mycrul—that's the other clone—because he was miserable without her. Now that she's here on Risda, you never see the two of them apart. Heard they work together, eat together, everything." He chuckles, shaking his head. "Can't say I'd be thrilled with having my female around all the time, but then again, I've never mated. Maybe it's different for some."

I want to shove a hand in his face to get him to stop talking. I have to think, and I can't think while he talks on and on. This makes no sense. A mate. The other clone of Crulden—Mycrul—has a mate. He gets to stay with her. He had his tusks removed so he could kiss her. Lord va'Rin even went off-world to purchase her to make Mycrul happy. They are together all day and everyone knows it, even this medic who runs his mouth and shares the secrets of others.

So...why am I being separated from Bee?

I straighten to my full height, squaring my shoulders. "Medic. I wish to speak to Lord va'Rin."

"And I wish for an assistant to do all this busy-work for me," he says with an amused chuckle, gesturing at his data pad. "You—"

"I wish to speak to Lord va'Rin," I state again. "I do not want to leave this place until I have spoken to him."

"That's not how this works, my friend—"

I raise a hand, silencing him. "If he has a marked interest in this Mycrul's happiness, he will have interest in mine. It is urgent that I speak with him." I nod at the comm station at the back of the small office. "Get on your machine and tell his people that Victor is here, and he has questions."

The medic stares at me for a long moment. Then, he sighs heavily and moves to the comm station. He taps the request onto the panel, then drums his fingers as it is sent. I know he feels he is wasting his time, and I am not surprised when, a moment later, he says, "He's not going to answer. He's an extremely busy man. He—"

The comm chirps with acceptance and a moment later, Lord va'Rin's face shimmers onto the screen.

The medic blinks in surprise.

I get to my feet, nodding at him. "Lord va'Rin. I have questions."

The mesakkah lord inclines his head. "Ask. I will try to answer."

I stalk toward the panel, wishing that this medic was not here to listen in, but I do not have time to chase this male away. There are other concerns at stake. "This Mycrul...he has a human mate?"

Lord va'Rin nods.

Hope surges in my chest. "What if I wished to stay with Bee? What if I did not want to go to the coast? Am I allowed to stay here in Port if she will have me?"

va'Rin looks surprised at my request. "Of course you may stay. I was under the impression that you wished to be far away from Port. That you preferred solitude." He leans in, studying my face. "In fact, one of the guardsmen said that you confessed to him that all you wanted was to get away from others. That you craved peace."

"I crave Bee," I say, shaking my head. "I do not care where I am, as long as I am with her. She is my mate."

The mesakkah lord narrows his eyes. "And does the female feel the same?"

"I would hope so. We have shared a bed for the last several weeks." The medic coughs in surprise, and I rush on. "But I will only stay if Bee haves me. If she does not want me, there is no need for me to remain here."

Lord va'Rin strokes his chin thoughtfully. He is silent for a long, long moment. "I was assured she had no feelings for you."

Who would tell him such a thing? We have carefully concealed our relationship from Herrix and Akris, but that was because Bee did not want our intimacy to reflect poorly on my training. "Did Novis say such a thing?"

"No, it was a male named Riffin—"

I growl before he even gets the words out. "Is he the male that said I loved privacy and wished to be far, far away from Bee?"

Lord va'Rin continues to stroke his chin. "You think he lied?"

"I think he wants Bee for himself."

"And who do you think she wants?"

"Me," I growl. "I am the best for her." I want to pour out all the ways I am the best mate for Bee, but this male is not the one I need to convince. I need to talk to Bee. I need to see if she truly wants me gone, or if her too-cheery smiles are her way of hiding how she feels.

She has been excessively smiley lately, now that I think about it.

"Then talk to her," Lord va'Rin says. "And if she wishes to be involved with you, have her contact me and let me know. And if you do not wish to go to the coast..." His smile grows cunning. "I know who can fill the spot perfectly."

I like the way this male thinks.

22

VICTOR

*I*nstead of waiting for Akris to return, I follow Bee's scent through town and pause in front of a building next to one with a sign written in human. I sound it out—*gee n rah sto re*. Oh. A store. A place where they sell things. And Bee is next to it—she'll like that. I move past the building and its strange scents, heading for the door that has my mate behind it.

I step inside and into an entryway. Waiting in the entryway is Akris, his mouth pressed into an unhappy line. Before I can ask, I hear voices. They mingle with the scents, and I pause, waiting.

"Riffin is here," Akris says unnecessarily. "Bee insisted on talking to him."

I nod and move closer to the wall. I don't enter. I listen instead to the sound of my female arguing with her former "boyfriend."

Riffin's hated scent is everywhere. Of course it is. He's wasted no time in moving in on my mate. More than that, I can hear his voice as he says something, and Bee responds. The walls here must be thick, because I can't make out their words. So I press my ear to the wall, because I want to hear everything.

"I thought you'd be pleased," Riffin is saying. "This office is what you wanted, isn't it? But you don't look happy."

"Just...go away. I'm really not in the mood."

"Because of that creature?"

"He's a person, not a creature." There's a strange note in Bee's voice. "And I'm fine. But please leave."

"You're not fine." Pure annoyance is in Riffin's tone. "You look as if your world has ended. Surely you're not sad that he's leaving?"

"So what if I am?"

She is? My heart thuds. Perhaps she cares for me, too. Perhaps all of Bee's smiles have been nothing but her hiding her feelings, as I wondered.

"Why? I'm willing to take you back. I'm willing to try again, Bee. You and I—"

Bee makes an outraged sound. "There is no you and I, Riffin! I don't love you. I love Victor. Him leaving hasn't changed that."

She loves me? The ache in my chest eases, replaced by joy. My Bee wants me.

"You can't love him." Riffin makes a disgusted sound.

"I can and I do. He's wonderful and smart, and clever, and so very tender."

"Do *not* tell me of his tenderness! I can still smell your cunt, you know. I should be revolted that touching him makes you react. Do I need to be more savage? Is that what it is?"

I curl a fist in anger, and the only reason I don't shove my fist through the thick wall to grab at Riffin's throat is because Bee laughs. Her laughter is sweet and pure and light. "You're just as clueless today as you've always been. It's not "savageness," as you like to call it. It's because Victor listens to what I say. He pays attention to what I need...which is something you'll never learn. And it doesn't matter, because...he's leaving." Her voice hitches, and I can hear the pain in her words. She sounds hoarse, as if fighting back tears. "It's...it's for the best."

"Is it? I've half a mind to go to Lord va'Rin and tell him your feelings for—"

"Don't you fucking dare," Bee's voice turns dangerous. "I will not have you ruin this for him! He has worked so hard to be trustworthy, and if you tell anyone about me and Victor, that'll ruin things. It'll cast doubt on him. They'll think he's just 'tamed' because of me, and I won't ruin this for him." Tears threaten her voice. "He deserves the very best...so you keep your mouth shut."

"Or what? What do I get in return?" The male's voice is smug, as if he's been waiting to corner Bee with his words all along.

I growl. He doesn't get a prize from her. Only I get her prizes.

"You can't," Bee protests. "You cannot sabotage this! He needs it—"

I've heard enough. I push off the wall, my fists clenched. I have to remember not to lose my temper. Any sign of aggression from me would reflect poorly in so many ways. Even though I want to tear Riffin's stupid face off, I have a better, far more pleasing idea of how to solve this situation. I step through the automatic doors, and my senses fill with Bee's scent and her soft sound of surprise. The office is small, with large windows, multiple boxes full of various goods, and an oversized desk across from the back wall. Bee stands in front of the desk, her hands on the surface behind her, and Riffin stalks near the windows.

Perfect.

"Victor...what...what are you doing here?" There's a terrified note in her voice as she pushes off the desk. Her worried eyes move over me. "What's wrong?"

"Nothing's wrong," I reassure her, crossing the room to her side. The moment I do, I tip a finger under her chin, forcing her to look up at me. "I wanted to look at your beautiful face again."

Her lips part. I can see the confusion on her face as she tries to understand why I'm here in her office instead of at the clinic. "Oh, uh." She glances over at Riffin. "I didn't know you'd be back so early."

She's probably wondering just how much I heard of the conversation. Of Riffin threatening her. Of Bee confessing her love for me and how she's keeping it to herself because she wants everyone to think the best of me.

You cannot sabotage this, she'd said to Riffin desperately.

Such foolishness. As if I have ever cared about the opinions of anyone except her. She worries that her affection for me— her love—will prevent anyone from trusting that I am reformed. When will she realize that doesn't matter if I don't have her? That I do not care what happens to me if I am not with her?

So I smile down at my sweet, small, worried mate. I run my thumb along the line of her rounded jaw...and then I grab her by the hips and haul her up onto the desk.

"Victor?" Bee asks, confused as she sits atop it. "What are you doing?"

"I am sabotaging things," I say, and step between her thighs. When she looks up at me, I slip my hand between her thighs and press my thumb at the spot where her clit peeks out from her folds.

Her lips part in surprise, and I duck down and capture her mouth in a hungry kiss. Near the window, Riffin makes a sound of disgust, but Bee goes soft under me. The scent of her drifts through the air, and I slick my tongue over hers in a silent promise. I lift my lips from her mouth and she gives me a dazed stare.

"I love you, too," I murmur. "Lean back for me."

She does so automatically, her hands bracing on the desk as she tilts her body backward. It makes those gorgeous, large teats of hers push out, but I'm more interested in something a little more showy. I drop to my knees in front of her, hitch her legs over the edge of the desk and onto my shoulders, and bury my face between her clothed legs.

Bee whimpers, her entire body trembling, because she knows what comes next. Her body floods with arousal, and I lick her through the fabric, my tongue pressing hard against her seam.

"What are you doing?" Riffin demands, his scent one of disgust, his voice full of panic. "Let her go."

I lift my head, running one tusk along the inside of Bee's thigh. "Do you want me to let you go?"

She swallows hard, then shakes her head. Her hand goes to my mane, and she curls her fingers in the strands, holding on tight. She's silently giving me permission, and my heart swells with pride. My female. *Mine.*

"What are you doing?" Riffin asks sharply again, taking a step forward.

I glance over at him, rubbing my tusk along the inside of her thigh again. "I'm sabotaging things. Did you want to watch me claim my mate on this desk? Because I assure you, your presence is not going to stop me."

Riffin makes a wordless protest, staring at me in horror. I turn back to Bee and nuzzle her cunt again, rasping my tongue along the seam of her trou so it pushes against her sensitive skin. Her breath catches, and even though she's trying to be quiet, a needy little sound escapes her.

"You are my mate," I tell her, focusing my attention entirely on Bee. I slide a hand under her tunic to the auto-fastener at her waist, loosening it with a touch. "You are my everything. I love you. I don't care where I am or what I do as long as I am with you."

"Animal," Riffin snarls, flinging himself toward the door.

I just grin. Animal? Perhaps to him. But all that matters is what Bee thinks.

"Victor," she breathes, her fingers scratching at my scalp as I tug on her clothing. I haul them down her thighs, exposing her skin and barely aware that Riffin is no longer in the room. My concentration is on Bee. I'm going to claim her in this office with my mouth, and then I'm going to get my barbs removed, and then I'm going to claim her in this office again. And again. And a dozen times over. "You...you shouldn't have done this. He's going to tell everyone."

"Let him." I tug her trou down far enough that the material pools at her knees. Close enough. I push her legs up in the air, exposing her cunt to my gaze fully as I put my hands on the backs of her thighs. "I spoke with Lord va'Rin. Did you know the other Crulden has a mate?" I tease my fingers up and down her damp slit, then gently push a finger into her channel. "And va'Rin approves?"

Bee makes a needy sound, her cunt clenching around my finger. "W-what? I don't understand."

I brace one arm over her thighs, pushing them toward her teats as I work her pretty cunt with my pumping finger. Akris is probably going to hear everything—Riffin, too, if he's loitering —but part of me wants them to hear it. I want them to hear how good I can make her feel. How hard I can make her come. I want to show the universe that she's mine. I want her to reek with my scent. I want every pore of her to be stamped with the fact that she belongs to me. I tongue her clit, sucking on the little bud until she cries out, her thighs trembling. "I'm going to lick this cunt," I tell her. "And you're going to scream my name. And I'm going to come all over those folds of yours and push my seed into your body with my fingers, because I want my scent all over you. Then we're going to have a comm with Lord va'Rin and you tell him how you really feel about me." I circle her clit with my tongue, flicking it lightly and enjoying the way her thighs jerk in response. "Then, if you want to be with me, I'm going to have the barbs removed from my cock, and we're going to live at the pump house, and we're going to be mates in every way possible. Because Lord va'Rin just wants quiet, and he doesn't care if I'm with you or if I'm on the coast, as long as we both agree to it."

She cries out, rocking her hips against my pumping finger with desperate need. "R-really?" she gasps, breathless. "He said that?"

"Mmmhmm." I don't lift my mouth from her clit. I keep sucking on it, working her cunt with my fingers because nothing else matters right now. Not the windows across the room, where someone can probably see my head under the hem of her skirted tunic as she writhes on the desk, her legs in the air. Not the fact that Riffin and Akris are listening in. Not the fact that this entire room is going to be coated in mating scent, and that when we leave here, everyone in town is going to know what we did. All that matters is making Bee come.

Her body shudders and she soaks my face with her release a short time later, crying out my name. I lick her pretty cunt clean, murmuring how good she was, how much I liked that, how much I ache for her. Instead of straightening her clothes, though, my naughty mate just wriggles her bare ass as I straighten. "Are you going to come?"

I groan. "Do...you want that?" I told her all kinds of filthy things when I was pleasuring her, but I mostly just want what she wants. If she's done, I am content. "Or are you too sensitive?"

"Rub the tip against me," she pants, her hands cupping her breasts as she gazes up at me. "Come on my pussy, like you said.

If we're going to do this, we're going to do it right. I'm going to wear your scent everywhere for the rest of my life."

Stars, but this female is perfect. I pull my cock free from my trou, gripping the barbed shaft beneath the head so I won't scrape anything against her. I drag the crown over her slick folds, fascinated at how good she feels. How slick and wet and ready. How it would take nothing for me to push into her and claim her.

"Soon," I breathe, rubbing the head up and down through her folds.

She reaches for her cunt and holds her folds open with two fingers, displaying herself for me. "Soon," she agrees. "I love you."

I come at that, at the yearning in her voice. Hot seed spills from my cock and I squeeze my shaft tight, gritting my teeth. The urge to pump, to add friction, is maddening, but I know Bee doesn't like it when I hurt myself. I spurt my release all over her inner thighs, fascinated as it drips over her supple skin and leaves thick trails. With a shiver, I shake the last of my load off the head of my cock, then use my fingers to rub it all over her cunt and into her body, just as I promised.

Soon.

23

VICTOR

*O*nce we've both come, I drag Bee off the desk, sit on the floor, and curl up with her in my arms. I nip at her throat and tease her ear as we touch and kiss and talk. "I thought that if I confessed how I felt about you," Bee tells me, "how I'd spent every night in your bed for the last few weeks, that no one would trust that you'd really been 'reformed.' They'd think I'd been dickmatized by you and tricked, and then they'd put you in a cage again." Her hand trails down the front of my tunic, my chokingly tight collar loosened. She gazes up at my face, her expression thoughtful. "I couldn't do that to you. If it meant I had to lose you for you to be happy, I was willing to do it."

"You weren't upset when Lord va'Rin suggested my departure," I point out. "I didn't know what to think."

"Victor." She cups my cheek, tangling her fingers in my thick, shaggy mane there. Sideburns, she calls them. "I've spent years and years hiding how I really feel about things. I've spent every day on this planet wearing a cheerful smile and sweet-talking every alien I run into because that's the only power I have. I turn back to that when I have to. But if you think for one moment that the thought of you leaving didn't gut me...you're wrong."

Her eyes meet mine and they're shiny with unshed tears.

"Don't cry." I rub my thumb over her cheek. "I can't stand the thought of you sad, Bee."

"I'm not sad now," she manages, blinking rapidly. She wriggles on my lap, a mischievous smile curving her mouth. "I'm content and loose and my pussy is wet with your seed. I don't think I've ever been happier."

I groan, because hearing that makes me happy, too. I run my nose along her brow, drinking in her scent mingled with my seed. It's chokingly thick in the room and I love it. I didn't think it was possible for her to smell better, but I'm addicted. "I can get my barbs removed at the medical clinic," I tell her. "The medic said it was a routine procedure...but it won't matter if I can't have you. Lord va'Rin said that the other Crulden clone has a mate. That he's fine with us being together, but you have to tell him that you want to be mine." I hesitate, wondering if I'm pushing too hard. "But...only if you want that."

She steers my face with her hand until I am facing her, and her smile is brilliant. "Of course I want that. Are you...all right with getting your barbs removed? I know it's a sensitive area."

"I want nothing more than to be inside you," I admit. Just the thought is making my cock rise again.

"What about the job at the shore? The garden?" She bites her lip, worried on my behalf. "I don't want to keep you from doing important work."

"My job is being your mate. Staying at your side. Protecting you." I take her hand in mine and rub my tusks against her knuckles lightly. "You want to help these females that have no one else to help them. Yes? You need someone to enforce this help. I can be that enforcer."

Her eyes widen. "You'd do that for me?"

"Bee, I would spend the rest of my life in a cage for you."

She frowns at that. "No cages. Never again."

"No cages," I agree.

"And no barbs." She leans in and kisses me, our mouths fitting together poorly as always, but I still love it. "No boundaries between us."

"None."

Her expression grows determined. "Then let's make a few calls."

To no one's surprise, Lord va'Rin is just amused at Bee's new suggestion for me to be her assistant/enforcer. We're to keep the pump house cottage, and he promises a faster air-sled so we can drive into Port with ease. I'm astounded at the male's generosity time and time again, but Bee says he has a human wife that he loves dearly, so that must be the reason behind his largesse. I'll take it.

We call the medic next to discuss my upcoming "procedure" and I'm a little nervous when he says we can return to his clinic today. That it's a simple "lasering" that won't take more than an hour and a few days of rest on my part. I've wanted this for so long, but now that it is here, I'm a little worried about getting such a pleasurable part of myself lasered. Bee is so enthused, though, that her excitement fuels mine. I want to be Bee's mate in all ways. Even if I have to get a cybernetic cock, I'll go through with it.

Anything for my mate.

24

BEE

I love Victor, but he's a terrible patient.

Then again, I probably would be, too, if I'd just had a bunch of spikes removed off a very sensitive part of my body. In the last four days, we've moved back into the pump-house, and the trunk has been unpacked. A new bed was delivered the next day, twice as large as the last and big enough that Victor doesn't have to sleep hunched up. Which, I suppose, is a good thing, since I've been sleeping on the far side of the bed.

The medic in Port said it was a routine procedure...for children. And he gave us a numbing salve that would help things, and told Victor to expect that area to be sensitive for a few days. The de-barbing was done, and a dopey, dazed Victor was sent back home with me. I tucked him into bed, made sure the bandages in his pants were fresh, and went back to sending recorded comm messages to the human women near Port to let them know I'm a case worker specifically seeing to the needs of the human settlers here, asking if they need anything and inviting them to come and visit my new office in Port.

When Victor woke a few hours later, he was groaning with pain. His cock was a fiery, angry red and swollen, and even though the medic assured us this was normal, it worried me. I slathered numbing cream on his cock as Victor hissed and twisted as if in agony, and when that didn't take the entire edge off, the medic came out in an air-sled and gave Victor a shot that made him loopy.

"The biggest ones are always the ones that can't take the pain," the medic griped. He handed me a handful of auto-injectors, advising me to keep Victor drugged if the discomfort persisted.

That was four days ago, and ever since then, I've been looking after my mate while he slept.

And slept.

And slept.

Really, it's not so bad. I worry about Victor more than anything, but the angry red has been fading steadily, and he's no longer swollen. I just hate that he's in pain, and I miss talking to him and cuddling with him. I've been afraid to touch him for the last few days out of fear that I'd brush up against something. The house is clean, I'm caught up on all of my messages, and I've even received a few from Lord va'Rin, checking in on us.

His last message was particularly delightful, despite its brevity.

Riffin is now assigned to the coast. He should trouble you no longer.

A small, evil part of me is delighted. I read the message again as I sit in front of the comm, smiling to myself as I sip my tea. I'm going to have to figure out how to save that particular missive. Maybe I'll embroider it and hang it on the wall. Maybe—

"Bee," a familiar voice groans from the bedroom.

I get up immediately. "Coming," I call out, grabbing the nearly empty jar of salve and the injectors just in case. Poor Victor. He'd been so excited to get rid of the barbs—I had too—and all of the excitement has disappeared with the pain he's gone through. If he's afraid to touch his cock for a month, I wouldn't blame him.

But that's all right. As long as he's not hurting, I'll do whatever it takes. As long as we're together, that's all that matters to me.

I peek into the dark bedroom and the bed is still occupied. "I'm here," I say softly. "Do you need pain meds? Food? Water?"

Victor groans again, reaching a big hand out for me.

Oh dear. I immediately slip my free one into his grip. "I hate that you're still hurting. I can't believe—"

My words die in a yelp as Victor drags me into the bed and I fall onto my back. He immediately nuzzles at my neck, his tusks brushing against my skin, and his tongue flicks at the sensitive spot where my shoulder meets my throat. Something big and hard and prominent pushes against my thigh.

"Hello, mate," my big alien purrs against my skin. His hand paws at my breast, seeking my nipple. When he finds it, he immediately plucks at it, teasing it into a point. "Guess what feels better today?"

"A whole heck of a lot, I'm guessing," I tease back. I rub my breast against his palm, because he feels so good and I've missed his touch. "No pain?"

"None," he agrees, kissing down my throat. An impatient hand tears at my tunic. "And you are far too clothed."

I chuckle, worming out of his grasp. "I love you, but you need to shower and eat before we get frisky."

Victor immediately drags me back into bed the moment I get free. "Mate now, eat later."

I push lightly at his chest. "Bathe and eat now," I say firmly.

"For one, you've eaten hardly anything in days and you need your strength. And two—I've been putting salve all over that cock of yours for the last few days and if it has numbing properties, I don't want it inside me. Understand?"

That makes him pause. He groans, burying his face against my neck again and snuffling. "Fine," he murmurs. "Bathe now. Shove food into mouth. Then mate my female."

Happiness clogs my throat, preventing words. He feels better, and we can be together. I don't think I've ever wanted anything so badly, and to realize that my dreams are coming true is overwhelming. When he holds onto me for a bit longer, I stay in his arms, just because I can. Just because it's the place I'm meant to be.

After a few minutes of uninterrupted snuggling, though, Victor's lazy kisses grow insistent. "Shower," I remind him with a pat. "I'll make you something to eat."

I head into the kitchen, my happiness still bubbling over. That happiness slides into amusement when Victor's shower seems to go on for forever. I'm guessing that he's touching that newly smoothed cock of his just because he can. Part of me wants to jump into the shower and interrupt (or help out), but I give him time, instead. If I had strange changes to my private areas, I'd probably be exploring them too.

If nothing else, I'd want to make sure everything was working properly.

So I sit as patiently as I can and try not to think too much about sex. About how Victor had his cock modified for *me*, and about how he's going to take me into our bed and push his big, thick length into me for the first time. He's going to fill up all the empty, aching places that I try to ignore when we touch each other, and even though I try to focus, I'm still thinking about sex after all. I imagine him touching himself, stroking his shaft, his taut mouth open just slightly with the wonder of how good it feels. Is he squeezing as he strokes? Or is this all new to him? I picture him pleasuring himself, and it takes everything I have not to get up and rush into the lavatory to "assist."

I press my hands between my thighs and I'm not surprised to find myself wet. So much for not thinking about sex. By the time the water shuts off, I'm practically squirming in my chair. The door to the lavatory opens and Victor steps out, a towel around his hips, his expression dazed. His nose twitches as he moves forward, and then his gaze locks on me. "Bee..."

"Feel better?" I ask, my voice husky.

He groans, moving toward me. I jump to my feet, breathless with anticipation, and when he scoops me up in his arms and the towel drops to the floor, my heart flutters with excitement. "I can smell your need," he growls, hitching my body up against his chest as he hefts me up by the buttocks. "It's perfuming the entire house."

"I was trying to be patient," I tell him, wrapping my arms around his neck and pressing my breasts to his wet front. I don't even care that he hasn't toweled off all that well. He's here and he's mine and I want him. "But then I figured you were touching yourself in the shower and I couldn't stop thinking about that, and it turned me on."

"You should have joined me," Victor says as he crosses into the bedroom. "I would have welcomed it."

"I wanted you to be the first one to give it a test drive. Does it feel good?"

The sound he makes is so erotic, my toes curl. "Sensitive," he rasps, laying me down on the bed. "So keffing sensitive."

"Then it'll feel good when you finally take me, won't it?" I sit up on the bed, putting a hand to his damp chest. He's naked, the towel forgotten in the living area. "But you should eat first."

Victor shakes his head. "Claim my mate. Then eat. I've waited long enough."

I'm about to argue, but the heated need in his gaze sweeps

the breath from my lungs. "Are you...so soon? Do you need a moment?"

"I need you," he says hungrily. He puts a hand on my shoulder, pushing me back onto the bed, and kisses me. His mouth is urgent, his tongue demanding as he licks into my mouth, claiming me for his own. All his need is in his kiss, and when he moves over me, I can feel the prod of his cock against my leg.

That didn't take long at all. He's hard as stone already.

When his mouth lifts from mine, I nip at his lower lip, as ravenous for more as he is. "Okay, you've convinced me. Sex now, please."

He grins, then leans in to kiss me again. The moment he does, he slips his hand into the loose waist of my pants and seeks my pussy. I'm wet and slippery already, and when he groans against my mouth, I pant with sheer need. "How did you ever think you were unable to get aroused? Look at how wet you are for me."

"I guess I needed a champion." I rock against his fingers. "Help me undress?"

Victor's eyes flare with hunger, and he grabs at my tunic. Quickly, I realize he's impatient enough that I'm going to end up with a lot of ripped clothing, so I squirm out from under him, undressing as I go. My tunic is a pretty pink one with embroidered flowers and a delicately scalloped hem and I want to keep it. Pretty, feminine tunics are part of my armor.

I get to my feet, stripping, and Victor is right there with me, his hands all over my body. I moan with impatience, undressing as quickly as possible. When I shimmy my pants down my thighs, Victor grabs my hips and rubs his cock against my backside, and I nearly fall on the bed with how good it feels. My knees get weak, and I practically stumble out of my pants, kicking them aside. "Do that again."

"Bee...stars, you feel so keffing good. I've imagined taking you a hundred different ways, but I never thought it'd feel so keffing intense." He drags his cock against the cleft of my buttocks again, and it makes me want to squirm with just how badly I need him, need this. I move forward slightly, my hands on the edge of the bed as I angle my backside into the air.

"Want to do it like this?" I ask, breathless. "From behind? Or do you want face to face?"

"I want all of it," he groans, sounding pained with need. One big hand skims up my spine, then hauls me back to rub my bottom against his cock again. "You pick. I can't think. Just... need to be in you already."

Oh god, I want that, too. I want that so bad I'm trembling. So I climb forward on the mattress, get on my hands and knees, and tilt forward, thrusting my ass into the air, presenting to him. "Please."

"*Bee.*" The way he says my name is pure desire. As if he's going to lose his mind if he has to wait another moment to have me. I shift my weight, spreading my knees apart, and when I feel the press of his cock against the entrance to my core, I want to weep with how good it feels. Just the head of him is hard and thick, and we've played like this several times before—where Victor would dip the tip inside me and make me come just from that, but it felt too dangerous to do often. Now, though, he can push in as deep as he wants. He can take me as hard as he wants.

And I want everything he can give me.

Victor pushes the head of his cock into me, then slowly pushes further in. I knew the first time we had sex there wouldn't be a ton of foreplay, that he was going to need me so badly that it was going to be quick and messy. I didn't anticipate how much I'd need him, though. How I'd feel primed for a quick, dirty taking, as if the last few weeks have been nothing but a build-up to this moment. How much my heart would swell with love when he pushes inside me and his breath hitches in his throat.

"Tight," he manages.

"I can take you," I promise him. "Keep going."

His body presses against mine and I can feel Victor trembling, overwhelmed with sensation or from holding himself back. Maybe both. All I know is that it feels as if he's spearing me, his cock thicker than I'd imagined, and yet so good I want to just revel in the sensation. My fingers twist in the blankets and I bite back a moan as his hips jerk and he thrusts a little deeper. "Tell me," he chokes. "Tell me if you need to stop. You're so small and tight—"

"You feel amazing," I pant, turning my head to the side and pressing my cheek to the blankets so he can watch my expression. "God, you feel so good. I need this. Need you, Victor."

"Bee," Victor says, my name beautiful on his lips. "Bee. My Bee."

And he surges forward, sinking to the hilt with one snap of his hips.

I gasp, the sensation rippling through me. I exhale, feeling stuffed to the gills, and the stretch of him takes my breath away. It's verging on painful, but the sensation is so sharp that it's incredible, and when he freezes, I make a sound of wordless protest. "That was so good," I tell him, dazed. "Don't stop. Oh, don't stop."

Victor grips my hips tightly, his fingers digging into my extra padding. "Kef me," he grits out. "*Kef.* Kef *me.*"

"Victor," I whimper. I'm tearing the sheets off the bed but I don't care. I just need him to start moving inside me. To fuck me hard with that big cock of his. I close my eyes, my lips parting. "You feel incredible."

He growls low, the sound dangerous, but it just makes my toes curl with desire. I know he'd never hurt me, never lose control when it comes to me. That's a growl of delicious need, and when he moves his hips, burying himself deep again, I cry out his name. I knew sex with Victor—penis-in-vagina sex—

would be intense, but I just didn't realize how intense. His body shakes, and I know he's holding himself back. I open my eyes, glancing back at him over my shoulder. "Are you okay?"

His face is taut, his hands gripping my thick hips tight. Victor's face is all intensity, and he looks moments away from snapping.

"Victor?" I ask again softly.

"So much," he manages to grit out. "It's so much to feel you like this."

"Do you want to stop?"

The growl returns. "Never. Never, Bee." His throat works, and then he manages, "Need you so hard." His body jerks again, the movement tight, as if he's forcing himself to stop what he naturally wants to do. "Just...give me a moment..."

"Then take me hard," I tell him, and I clench my inner walls, squeezing as tight as I can. "I'm all yours."

The sound Victor makes is broken, as if he's been unleashed from whatever restraints he's put upon himself. Before I have time to say anything else, he slams into me again, hard and fast. I squeak, startled, but hot pleasure rushes through my body, making my skin prickle in response, and my sound of surprise turns into a moan. He lets out another broken noise and thrusts deep again. Then, he's driving into me with ruthless force, as if he's unable to stop himself. Over and over, he thrusts into me, my body (and the bed) shaking with the ferocity of his need.

And it feels so damned *good*.

With a little cry, I brace my elbows into the bed, trying to stop from sliding across the mattress. He's got my hips gripped tight, but the force of our mating is rattling the frame itself. I've never been fucked so hard, and the choked, gasping sounds I make somehow turn into pleading for more. More of his cock, more of his power, more of everything. I love it, and I love how he's losing himself in my body. I knew this would be so good, because we love each other, but god, I had no idea that I would need this so badly. I had no idea that when he bottomed out with each rough thrust, that the slap of his hips against my skin would send ripples of ecstasy through my body, or that he'd go so deep that it'd start a new, strange sort of hunger unfurling in my belly. All I know is that the moment that new wave of sensation hits me, I chase it. I slide a hand under my body and touch my clit, and as soon as I do, my body locks up in the hardest orgasm ever. I whine even as I touch myself, my body clenching tight around his driving cock, and when I come, I come so hard that I see stars and every muscle stops working, tight as tripwire. The climax races through me as I clench and squeeze, helpless to participate as he pounds into me and tells me how good I feel.

Then Victor is coming too, his breath stuttering as his movements jerk and lose their rhythm. I feel the hot pulse of him deep inside me, the warmth of his release surprisingly noticeable. His body temperature must be higher than mine, I think in a daze as his thrusts slow, the sound of him plunging into my body becoming wet and loud. I moan again, my eyes fluttering closed. Victor lets out a ragged breath and then collapses on top of me, his big body covering mine.

"Heavy," I murmur as he pushes me into the mattress. I don't move, of course. I'm too boned to move. He's dicked all the strength out of me.

Victor lets out a satisfied sigh, then gets off of me. His cock slides free from my sprawled body, and I let out a little sound of protest. I already want him back. He strokes his hands over my hips and thighs, then rolls me over and adjusts me like a doll, making me comfortable in the bed. "My beautiful Bee," he murmurs, gazing in fascination down at my body. His hand goes between my thighs, and he rubs my folds, slicking his fingers through the mess we've made and rubbing it all over my pussy. "I should have asked if I could come inside you. I didn't think."

"It's all right," I say, yawning. I'm always sleepy after a good round of sex and right now, I'm definitely feeling replete and in need of a nap. "You can't make me pregnant without medical assistance."

"Mmm. And do you want to be?" He glances up at me even as his wet fingers stroke over my skin.

I haven't really thought about it. "Maybe at some point? Right now I'm just happy we're together."

His smile broadens. "I am the same." Two fingers push inside me, and I wriggle against his hand. "But...I am glad I can come inside you. It was...so good, Bee." Victor's expression is dazed. "In all my imaginings, it was never as good as that."

I have to admit, I'm pretty speechless, too. I've had good sex before, but it's been a while. I've had good sex with Victor, but without penis. This good-sex-with-Victor-and-penis has kinda blown me out of the water. Despite his days of pain, I'm so very glad he's gotten his barbs removed. I roll over on my side toward him, my thighs trapping his hand in place. He's slid down on the bed so our faces are almost even, and I wrap my arms around his neck, leaning in. "I love you, and that was amazing."

His hand continues to move between my thighs, as if he can't stop touching me. After weeks of being with Victor, I know that he's very tactile, and I don't mind in the slightest. I ride his hand, squirming a little closer. "I...everything is really sensitive," he admits. "I wanted to last longer for you."

"It was perfect," I tell him, rubbing my small human nose against his bigger, alien one. "And we have a lifetime to figure out how to make things last longer. I'm in no rush."

Victor's breath fans over my face, his gaze searching mine. "I...might need to do it again. Very soon. Like in a few minutes."

I glance down, surprised, because we haven't even cleaned

up yet. Sure enough, his cock is growing hard once more. Alien stamina is really something else...or maybe he's just a champion in this, too. "Are you hungry? You still haven't eaten."

"I'd much rather claim my mate," he tells me, and his thumb grazes over my ultra-sensitive clit.

My legs jerk in response and I whimper. "I...suppose we can do that, too."

EPILOGUE

VICTOR

A collar. Again. "You're trying to kill me," I complain to my mate as she sits atop the back of the air-sled, fussing with the neck of my finest tunic. "I can't breathe in this thing."

Bee just rolls her eyes and smooths the auto-fastener into place with a touch. "You were fitted for this tunic, Mr. Drama. I know very well the neck fits. But if you want to change, let me know and we'll turn around right now and take the air-sled back to the house."

"It's fine," I grumble, because we had to drive fast to get here anyhow. Bee gets airsick when I drive, because my foot is heavy on the pedals. I try to make the drive faster, knowing it makes her stomach upset, and I only succeed in making her even more queasy. I feel guilty, but Bee says she prefers I drive, because she wants me to get used to doing everything. I suspect it's because she likes to talk and check her messages as I drive, and gets distracted.

My Bee does love to talk. In the two months since our official mating, I don't think Bee has gone an hour without talking.
I don't mind it, as there are few things I love more than Bee's
voice. I love it when it's raised in anger, when it's soft and husky,
when she's being managing and overly sweet, and most of all,
when she makes that little cry when my cock pushes into her.
Her voice just makes me happy.

She pats my collar, satisfied, and then smooths a lock of my
mane back from my brow. Her gaze moves over me. "So
handsome."

I snort at that, but I'm secretly pleased. I like that Bee finds
me good to look at, that her pulse speeds up when she watches
me. I don't care if I seem strange to everyone else, or that my
tusks make some in Port stare with horror. Bee likes my face,
and that's all that matters.

"Can you get the casserole?" Bee asks me as she hops down
from the trunk of the air-sled and straightens her own clothes.
She's wearing a pair of beige, silky trou under her pale yellow
tunic with the deep collar that shows off her amazing cleavage
and a thick, wide belt that clasps her waist and emphasizes her
curves. Her dark curls are perfect, pulled back behind each tiny
rounded human ear with a pretty clip. Her skin glows with
health and best of all, she is positively covered in my scent. She
looks beautiful, and I'm tempted to climb back into the air-sled,
pull her into my lap, shove her trou down and seat her onto my
cock...it wouldn't be the first time we'd mated in the air-sled. In
fact, I suspect half of Port has seen us stumble out of the sled,
clothing disheveled and the windows of the sled steamed and
foggy.

I retrieve the food dish from the sled itself and glance over
at my mate. "I still don't know why we're bringing food to Lord
va'Rin. He can afford to feed himself."

"It's called 'manners,' Victor. When I grew up, you didn't
visit company without bringing a dish. Doesn't matter how rich

the company is." She smiles up at me with that delightful, managing smile of hers and loops her hand into the crook of my arm. "And you're just fussing because you're nervous to meet Mycrul."

"Maybe," I grumble. "But...what if he wants to fight?" I don't know if I want to fight another version of myself. It is one thing to be my mate's protector and to guard her office, to loom threateningly over males that are abusing their females. We've had a few incidents since Bee started her job that have made me glad for my fearsome demeanor and massive size, because those keep most in line without having to resort to violence. But this Mycrul...I don't know what to think.

"He won't want to fight," Bee reassures me. "Mina says he's very gentle now. I told you he works with animals for a living, right? Mina said he's almost finished with the first level of testing to be an apprentice animal-medic. Stock-medic." Her nose wrinkles as she thinks. "Whatever they call it here. A veterinarian."

I grunt. "You sound proud of him."

She smacks my arm. "Be nice. The social worker in me is just pleased he has an outlet for his energy, like you."

Do I have an outlet? I think about my mate, and how she rode my tusks as I licked her cunt before work this morning and then laid her on her back and pumped her full of seed until she was crying out my name. It was rather enjoyable, now that she mentions it, but I do not see what it has to do with Mycrul and his animals. "I guess."

"Don't be nervous," she reassures me. "I talked to Mina a little and she said he's very excited to meet you."

Which is why we are heading to dinner at Lord va'Rin's estate, with a dish of stewed veg under my arm, in my most uncomfortable tunic, instead of reading a book at home with Bee and then making my mate come at least twice under my ministrations. "We shall see."

I am silent as we pass the guards, several of whom I recognize from my time in my cell, back before they let Bee come in to greet me. Those days seem very long ago, and I wonder what my life would be like if my female had not turned her charm on and decided that I needed a friend, and that friend was her. My life is completely different now, my days filled with guarding Bee and the humans that visit her, and my nights filled with pleasuring my mate and enjoying her company. I never even think of championships or gladiator duels.

Maybe that is why I am nervous to meet Mycrul, I think, as we are escorted in by a uniformed servant, dressed in the house colors and symbols of Lord va'Rin. I am happy and I do not want him to drag me into a life that I have unpleasant memories of but have never experienced.

As if she can sense my unease, Bee squeezes my arm. "It's going to be fine, love. Wait and see."

We step inside the grand foyer of Lord va'Rin's house, admire the artwork he has on display (including a large portrait of him, his small, red-haired mate and their equally small children), greet the lord and his mate when they arrive, and I hand the dish of food over to Milly va'Rin.

"Oh, you're so thoughtful, Bee. Thank you both." Milly beams at us as if we have given her a prize. "I'll just set this on the table. Mycrul and Mina are in the sitting room." She gestures at a pair of closed double doors and moves down the hall.

My collar turns chokingly tight. Lord va'Rin exchanges pleasantries with my mate, who squeezes my arm again and gestures at the room across from us. She's telling me without words that I should go inside and introduce myself. I press a kiss to the top of her head and then stride over to the double doors that must be the sitting room. Before I go inside, I can smell...myself, but not. It's strange. It's like me, but a slightly spicier scent and a different soap. There's also the smell of an unfamiliar female mingled with his.

I open the door and step inside.

There's a scrawny female sitting on one of the chairs. She has thick, slashing brows that seem huge in her small, pale face. It's the only noticeable feature about her, so I turn toward the male at the far end of the room. His hands are on his hips, his back to me, as he stares at a crystalline vase with a frown on his face. It's like he's no more comfortable here than I am.

I close the door and immediately, the male turns. His nostrils flare, and we stare at one another.

It's my face...but not. His mane is cut short, his jaw shaved. His tusks are gone, and he almost looks...civilized. Me, with all the edges filed off. It's strange, but I touch my own jaw and I'm glad that I kept my tusks. Do they pull at my mouth? Yes. Do they look fearsome? Also yes, and Bee loves them.

"Holy shit," the female says softly.

"You are Mycrul?" I say, taking a step forward. "I am Victor." Pain pricks at my back, as if my spikes are preparing to launch themselves through my skin. Bee told me that Mycrul would not want to fight, but I need to be ready if he does. I need to protect my mate.

As if we share thoughts, he immediately steps in front of his scrawny mate and sizes me up.

"Victor," he says slowly, as if tasting my name. His tail lashes, and his mate swats at it. "As in...winner? Have you battled many, then?"

I can smell the tension radiating off of him as he tries to keep his female behind him. It occurs to me that he has the same concerns I do—that he is worried I will be like Crulden and want to fight and harm—and that is why we are here at Lord va'Rin's estate instead of somewhere more private. "It is just a name," I admit. "Crulden did not fit me, so Bee suggested that one." I manage a half-smile. "She did not want to call me 'Asshole' like the guards did."

The female snorts with amusement.

Mycrul puts a hand behind him, and I see her fingers lace with his, even though his expression does not change. "Do you have his memories?" he asks. "Crulden's?"

"Some," I admit. "None of them good."

"Mine either." His mouth twitches, and then he smiles broadly, the sight of it pleasingly strange and unfamiliar without the tusks. He is a different person, and I am glad to see it. "Mina says I should focus on the future, not the past."

"Bee says something very similar," I admit. "But Bee also likes to tell people what to do."

Mycrul's mouth twitches again. "We noticed. She set up this meeting."

"I know. She wanted me to get to know you both." I love my mate with all my heart, but I know her better than anyone, and I know how much she loves to prod and manage people. "If you do not want to be here, I understand. I just want to live quietly with my mate at my side."

"We don't mind being here," the female says, her voice fierce. "Do we, Mycrul?"

The male wearing a face that is almost mine watches me and then nods slowly. "I thought it would be good to meet."

"My Bee wants us to be family," I admit, since she will be in here in a moment and tell them just that. My collar is tight and I feel awkward and strange. As I watch, Mycrul adjusts his own collar, and it makes me feel a little better. "Just so you know."

I expect the male to laugh in my face. To show his fangs, like the Crulden of my memories would. To display his claws and then use them on every surface—and every person—available. But Mycrul only gives me that strange, tusk-less smile and squeezes his scrawny mate's hand. "It would not be a bad thing to have family."

I smile back, because like me, he is not Crulden. He is his own person. "Family would be good."

"If we are family, then can I unfasten my collar?" Mycrul asks, glancing down at his mate as he tugs at it with his free hand.

I let out a huge sigh and free my own, rubbing my throat. "Thank the stars for that."

Mycrul stares at me and then throws back his head and laughs.

It's almost the same laugh as mine. Almost, but not quite, and when I join in, it feels good to laugh. We are family, after all.

AUTHOR'S NOTE

Hello there!

I decided this book would come about almost immediately after I finished BAD GUY. I had SO much fun with that book that I knew I wanted to write another. I hope you enjoyed it! I don't think I have plans for more Crulden clones just yet, but never say never! There might be an Ultimate Bad Guy lurking on some distant station, just waiting for his own book. You never know. I also thought this would be just a short novella... but I'd also thought the same thing about BAD GUY and we all know how that turned out. Basically if I call it a novella, you can expect 200 pages at this point.

(I really need to stop doing that to myself...)

I feel like this book fits pretty closely in the Risdaverse general scheme of things - you don't have to have read everything else to follow along, really. It just helps fill in some of the blanks if you have. If you're wondering about timeframes, this book occurs in the period just after BAD GUY finishes.

I loved writing Mycrul and Mina so much that I was actually tempted to write Victor and Bee into a similar situation...

except I also realized immediately that wouldn't work. For one, I've established that Lord va'Rin is a good guy, if overworked and delegating a lot (hence First Rank Novis). It wouldn't make sense for his guards to be abusive. Trigger happy and clueless? Yes. Unable to get along with Victor/Crulden? Yes. But downright mean? No. Victor is caged and cuffed because he can't stop lashing out, so it's due to his own actions and a policing force that has no clue what to do with a very violent man they're supposed to reform. His head is filled with angry, piecemeal memories, and that's all he has to establish his personality. It isn't until Bee comes in and treats him like a person instead of just a problem that he starts to blossom into his own self.

Bee is very different from Mina, as well. Whereas Mina was the grudgiest slave ever (who wouldn't be?), Bee has been freed for a while, but the scars of her captivity still hang over her. She's learned to cope with her lack of power by manipulating everyone around her with smiles. In a way, it made me think of the Southern saying of 'Bless your heart' which sounds so very nice until you realize the person saying it isn't intending for it to be nice at all. Bee is nice, but she also likes to get her way. I thought it was a fun angle for a heroine to reclaim her power, especially one that's been through what she has.

I also liked the idea of a marriage of convenience being absolutely wrong for both parties involved! I've had so many happy convenience-marriages on Risda that I wanted to show one that wasn't so great. Bee is using Riffin for the protection a relationship with an alien provides, and Riffin is using Bee for kissing and showing off to his friends. He doesn't love her - he just loves the status she gives him. Luckily neither party was even close to making it official, so I didn't feel too bad about breaking them up.

And of course, Mycrul and Victor meet, because they couldn't NOT meet, right? I liked writing a cozy, domestic little scene because it's just so different from what you'd expect from two fierce gladiators. But...I like different. :)

At any rate, I sincerely hope you enjoyed Victor and Bee's story. I'm sure this won't be the last of them. They'll be in Port, with Victor standing guard as Bee takes care of business for future heroines. :)

Much love,

Ruby

WANT MORE RUBY DIXON?

Need more to read? Allow me to make a few suggestions! All of my books are in Kindle Unlimited, so borrow away!

Want to read Mycrul's story?
BAD GUY

Want to read about Lord va'Rin and Milly?
PRETTY HUMAN

How about some Risdaverse?
RISDAVERSE TALES
WHEN SHE'S READY
WHEN SHE PURRS
WHEN SHE BELONGS

Or maybe you're in a barbarian sort of mood?
ICE PLANET BARBARIANS

Enjoy!!

Printed in Great Britain
by Amazon